GLORIOUS & FREE

BRYCE DYMOND

Suite 300 – 990 Fort Street
Victoria, BC, Canada V8V 3K2
www.friesenpress.com

ISBN
978-1-4602-5138-6 (Hardcover)
978-1-4602-5139-3 (Paperback)
978-1-4602-5140-9 (eBook)

1. *Juvenile Nonfiction, Social Issues, Homelessness & Poverty*

Distributed to the trade by The Ingram Book Company

TABLE OF CONTENTS

To Evelyn, May you always live out your convictions.

ACKNOWLEDGEMENTS

THERE WERE MANY DAYS IN WRITING, LIKE in training for the One Nation Run, where I was by myself. If you can imagine it, it took me more time to write this book than it took for me to run across Canada with my friends. Similar again to the run, I could not have written this book without an army of support and inspiration, although by myself, I was never alone.

Firstly, I want to thank Zaya, who gave me the challenge of writing the book. My brother, you are a great inspiration and you help keep my eyes on that which is most important. As the better writer, I hope, one day, that you have the good fortune and discipline to write your own book: I will be the first in line to read it. In thanking Zaya, I cannot forget to thank Brittany and all those who ran, housed, fed and cheered us on. You ensured the team got to Vancouver with a strong stride. Brittany: you allowed Zaya and I to do what we do best, run and speak. As you worked hard behind the scenes, you shone brightly. Your role in the mission was just a vital as ours. Thank you, sister!

Thirdly, to my parents Brian and Sharon: from the moment I entered the world, you both instilled in me the belief that I was needed in Canada. As I got older, you trusted me to speak and live in such a way that I could impact people positively. When I doubted whether I should lead the run and write this book, your voices reminded me that I could. Thank you so much. I hope to empower and nurture Evelyn in the same way.

To Thom Anderson: thank you for your patience, interest and imagination toward this project. I was not sure if we were going to get past the first draft, but your creativity and encouragement lifted my vision to a higher place.

Kristen Rose: thanks for putting in crazy hours at the end of long work nights and weeks to edit this book before it made its way to FriesenPress. It was a laborious and tedious task and you did it with such skill and a generous spirit.

Thank you as well to FriesenPress. Thank you for your diligence in refining this book with me and for coordinating meetings with me despite being three time zones west. Your work will give this story a larger audience and give the One Nation Run team a treasure we can hold on to and share with our children.

To the World Vision Canada team: thank you for being an organization that I can trust, and about which I can be excited. Your work in Canada gives so many brave Canadian leaders the chance to give hope to vulnerable children and families going through turbulence. Thanks specifically to Genevieve Barber, Cynthia Koch, Elizabeth Goncalves, Charmain Sherlock, Hugh Brewster, Danny MacKay, Michael Messenger and Dave Toycen.

To my friends and family who invested in this project and promoted it to your circles, thank you. It was fitting that I needed your help yet again in sharing the story of the One Nation Run. It felt so good to achieve another goal with you.

To Rick and Liz Greer: your endurance and courage pushed me to serve the interests of others before my own selfish desires. Thank you for giving Brittany, Zaya, myself and so many more, a tangible example of sacrifice and for giving us the opportunity to meet the children of Central Manitoba.

I would not have run across Canada if I did not come face to face with Amy and the dozens of children I met in Central Manitoba. This book is about you and how you changed my friends and I. Your stories will lead many people to greater heights of humility and compassion and will make Canada even greater. Thank you for the beautiful exchange of friendship.

Lastly, to my wife Catherine, who literally suffered with me for the last three years while I worked on this project: your ears nearly fell off as you listened to me read draft after draft of the book to you and hear recaps of all the brainstorming sessions with Thom. I am still amazed that you gave me the gift of time and space to write the book while being unemployed, and all within our first year of marriage. This gift was something our accountants thought was nuts, but you always believed the project was worth the sacrifice. Thank you for being my partner in life and for sharing my love for Canada.

FOREWORD by Amelia Carver

*"Overcoming poverty is not a task of charity, it is an act of justice.
Like Slavery and Apartheid, poverty is not natural. It is man-made
and it can be overcome and eradicated by the actions of human
beings. Sometimes it falls on a generation to be great. YOU
can be that great generation. Let your greatness blossom."*

– Nelson Mandela

O CANADA! I HAVE ALWAYS BEEN PROUD TO
be a Canadian. Canada has a great reputation worldwide of being
friendly, beautiful and abundant. When people think of Canada,
they don't think of poverty or scarcity. They associate it with
richness, unity and freedom. While growing up I have always felt
very lucky to live in a country where all of its citizens live glorious and free – or so I thought. I'm embarrassed to say that I took
it so for granted.

After hearing about Bryce's goal to raise money for Canadian
children in poverty, I was initially a little confused. Why would
he need to raise money for *Canadian* children? When I learned
that one in ten children in Canada live below the poverty line and

i

thousands do not have access to clean drinking water, I was taken aback. This is unacceptable!

The problem is that like me, so many people are unaware of what is going on in their own country. When you consider Canada's reputation of being a land of plenty, I think it is quite surprising for many Canadians when they hear that 10% of children live in destitution. Not only was I taken aback, but I was upset that few people or charities dedicate their time and resources to helping solve this appalling issue. Mostly, I felt sad. It is not right!

When Bryce told me about the One Nation Run's goal to share the message that all children should be able to live glorious and free of poverty, I was very supportive of his plans and ideas and eager to help make a difference. Bryce's initiative made me excited to help bring awareness to others. He has reinforced my faith in Canadians and reminded me why I love it here so much. His compassion and eagerness have motivated and inspired me to make a difference.

Participating in the One Nation Run was a once in a lifetime experience that I will never forget! Seeing some of my friends, family and people I had never met before all running for an important cause, united from east to western sea, was invigorating and inspiring. It made me remember why I have always felt lucky to live in this beloved country. The movement sparked many young people across Canada to want to make their own difference, including me. I'm so grateful to have had the opportunity to learn from Bryce and to help out with such a worthy cause. Not only did Bryce affect the lives of children living in poverty, but he also affected the lives of people who want or need to be motivated to change the world.

I believe that by reading this book my peers will be reminded of how expansive and beautiful Canada is, but it will also open their eyes to the flaws our country is still working on, such as children in poverty. Bryce's story will challenge youth to have a vision and goals because he proved that one person can make a difference. My hope is that this book will continue to bring awareness and inspire Canadians of all ages to make a difference in our beloved native land so that Canada can truly be "glorious and free."

INTRODUCTION: Amy's Story

THE CLOCK ON MY CELL PHONE READ SIX IN the morning as the lights came on in the school gym. I woke up quickly while the rest of my teammates huddled in their sleeping bags. As I sat up, my back and neck were stiff – the effects of sleeping on a portable military cot. The gym was dry and dusty, and my nose was congested. It was not an ideal way to prepare for a gym day.

I began rolling up my sleeping bag and packing up my gear. Once cleaned up, my teammates and I would put our things in one of the school's classrooms for the day. We all could have used a shower to refresh ourselves, but soon we would be bringing equipment in from outdoors and the negative thirty degree temperatures would make us alert.

The conditions and cold, with the sun nowhere near rising, felt pretty far from a vacation, but that was exactly what my team members had given up to be there. They were mostly university students on their reading week. I was proud of them for making this trip a priority when their peers were sleeping in at home or on a beach somewhere in the Caribbean.

By 7:30 a.m. we had packed our gear and had moved the food from the van into the main lobby. We sat around cafeteria tables while Rick began toasting bagels. Liz, Rick's wife and the administrator of our gym day, set up a welcome and registration desk. Once the bagels were popping from the toaster, we gathered around the table, blessed the food and began eating. On the table there was milk, cereal, granola bars, apples, yogurt and juice. We would need a hearty breakfast to host the forty plus children who were coming to the school for the gym day.

While we ate, we talked about our sleeping conditions the night before. We were thankful that only two of our six sleeps that week would be spent in a gym on military cots. We went through the gym day's schedule: running games, relay races with "fruit tape", floor hockey and cup stacking (a favourite of the kids). It was a kid's dream day.

During breakfast, we sat laughing and talking, when suddenly we were startled by a knock at the door. We all stopped eating. We looked at each other wondering if it was a person at the door or the wind. It was 7:45 a.m. and no one was due to arrive until 10:00 a.m. The sun would not rise for another hour. Liz thought it might be the janitor coming to do his rounds. Rick thought it might be a school teacher coming to catch up on some marking on their day off. Then a second knock, but neither one of us could see a figure at the window. David, who was seated closest to the doorway, got up with Liz to see who or what it was.

They opened the door and looked down. Standing in front of them was a little girl. Liz knew her from past gym days.

"What are you doing here so early, Amy? The gym day does not begin for another two hours. Are you okay?" Liz asked.

"I know the gym day does not start 'til later, but I have not eaten for over a day," Amy replied.

As they spoke at the doorway, the freezing wind rushed in to the breakfast table.

Liz asked a second question, "How come you have not eaten? Where are mom and dad?"

"Dad is away this week for work and mom is at home. She's drunk."

All of us at the table stopped eating. We could not believe it.

Amy continued: "I came here now, because I knew you would be up having breakfast. I knew if I came you would have enough food for me, too."

Liz opened the door wider and brought Amy inside.

When Amy entered the school lobby and came closer to the table, it was obvious that she was freezing. She had been standing outside for 30 minutes before she had built up enough courage to knock on the door. She had not been wearing gloves; her hands were like icicles. When she sat down, another female teammate, Tristan, sat beside her. Amy was trembling, so she sat close to her as a source of body heat, while holding her hands to comfort her.

Many questions began to spring up in my head. I was feeling similar to how I felt just seven months ago in Little Saskatchewan. Because Amy was right across the table from me, I focused on her needs and not my emotions, but it was a wrestling match when it was quiet at the table for more than a few seconds. I wanted answers. Was this Amy's normal day-to-day or was it just because her dad was away and her mom had a bad week?

We continued to talk to Amy as she enjoyed the warmth and breakfast. I remember instantly becoming more aware of how fortunate we were to be having breakfast when Amy joined us. Tristan brushed Amy's hair back as she took off her coat. Amy's face became bright as she ate breakfast with us – transforming from cold and timid to warm and open. It was enough for the whole team to realize we were in the right place. I was in the most important place I could be.

I knew life for Amy was not ideal, but what she needed seemed so basic. It seemed bizarre to be eating a meal with a Canadian kid so desperate and lacking basic needs. During the course of the meal, I also noticed Amy was missing many of her teeth. Many of the teeth she did have were not in good condition. I could see her fillings reflect in the light.

The sun rose as we finished our breakfast and the light of the day entered the school's lobby. The team began cleaning up the table and then setting up sports equipment, ropes and cup stacking tables. Liz asked Amy to return home. She wanted to ensure that Amy's mom or siblings would not wake up in a panic because Amy was missing. Before she left, Tristan held her in a tight embrace. In a couple of hours, we would see Amy again, this time running around in the gym with a grin from ear to ear.

I realized that Amy's story was not unique in her community. Many homes that the children came from lacked stability and basic needs like heating, clean drinking water and proper nutrition. What was even sadder was that there was little for them to do after school. Our gym day was like an amusement park coming to town. All the children aged five to twelve joined us that day, parents even snuck in their four-year-olds. The children's stories cut into my heart and left a scar that would forever remain.

There were more disturbing facts about Amy's life that I discovered. In her community, healthy food like milk and produce cost two to three times the price people paid in other parts of Canada. The high prices meant Amy's parents could only afford things like chips, pop and frozen pizzas. The low nutritional value of this food meant that Amy and other children like her suffered from poor health.

Poor health, poor nutrition and an unstable home environment were not the conditions Canadian children should be living in. I could not believe kids in Canada – one of the richest nations in the world – were living like this.

Amy's story prompted me to ask many questions. What could I do? Would I act or just talk about being an advocate? Amy's story needed to be carried across Canada. But would I be the one to carry it? If so, how would I carry it? How many other communities in Canada looked like this? And how many Canadians were aware of their conditions?

But even before I met Amy, I had visited remote communities like hers. I knew that Amy's story was not isolated even though her community was. I had felt this tension and frustration before.

I did not want Canadian children to feel alone. Despite things like cell phones and the internet, communities like Amy's were not connected to the rest of Canada in a way that their story could be heard.

This book is a story about the children of Canada. It is about the most vulnerable children in Canada and how far they would inspire me to go. This book is about the hope that in the next generation, no Canadian children will ever have to live in poverty.

Above all, this book is an invitation. I want you to care more about your country and the children who live in it regardless of what differences you might have with them. There is a proverb that says, "It takes a village to raise a child." I believe in that proverb. I also believe that as it takes a village to provide for children, it takes a nation to provide for all of its children. With you it is possible. Without you it is not.

CHAPTER ONE: The Flag Pulled Over My Eyes

I WAS ON A FLIGHT TO WINNIPEG, MY MIND still coming to terms with the purpose of the trip. Around me, my teammates were sleeping, taking advantage of the two and a half-hour flight. The six of us would be spending a week co-leading a day camp for 40 to 50 children, all aged five to twelve in rural Manitoba. The group I was with was a group from the church I was working at, I was a pastor to youth and young adults. The group I was a mix of adults and young adults in their 20s.

As the plane ascended to its flying height, I continued to contemplate the trip. A few months earlier, two senior staff members had asked me to go. Although I respected their authority, I did not understand their logic. They had each gone a couple of times and said it was my turn. They believed I needed this experience.

When I was in high school, my best subject was history. I was no expert, but I believed I knew Canada's story pretty well. I learned about the courier du bois and Nelly McClung. I studied the War of 1812 and the Halifax Explosion. I saw pictures and watched movies that revealed the beauty of Canada from as far as the three ocean coasts. I wrote papers on Confederation and the cross-Canada railway. I was proud to be Canadian, and I was confident that my teachers had thoroughly educated me about my nation.

While I was on the plane, I was confused. What else could my superiors possibly want me to know about Canada? Was there something they believed I had not been taught? Along with my confusion was a touch of resentment. I thought my team's time would be better spent serving children in countries that were poorer than Canada.

My parents took my brother and I on a 56-day trip when I was nine. We travelled to ten different countries on three different continents. It was a life-shaping trip. For the first time in my life, I saw children living in terrible conditions. I saw children taking showers under rooftop spouts when it rained, for lack of indoor plumbing. I saw children swimming in rivers full of dead animals. I saw children forced to work because their parents were not paid enough at factories to cover their expenses.

Later in my life I traveled to Rwanda and while there I talked to a fifteen-year-old girl whose parents were killed in war. She took care of her household, as many other teenagers in her country did, their parents' lives cut short by disease and violence. As we talked, someone asked her what dreams she had for her future. Without hesitation, she responded: "Dreams? I do not have any dreams. I only try to help my family survive the day and the night."

In my adult years, I began to ask questions about how people lived the way they did and what could be done to see their conditions improve. With our plane now thousands of metres over Northern Ontario, I was finding it difficult to comprehend why our trip was destined for Winnipeg. Were there not other countries whose children needed our help and resources more?

Let me be clear, I knew there were needs in Canada. I knew there were children who needed mentoring and tutoring. I knew there were families who needed a little help paying the bills. I knew there were Canadian children who needed encouragement and protection. I was not blind to the fact that children in Canada had obstacles facing them. I was not deaf to the struggle that children in urban centres were going through. In fact, at the time of my trip to Winnipeg, I lived right down the street from a school that hosted a breakfast club for children who did not receive enough to eat in the morning. However, when it came to taking a short-term trip to make a concrete difference in another community, I thought my time would be better spent building schools and homes in a Third World country.

The plane began its descent, and the captain came on the intercom to tell us that we were close to Winnipeg. I looked around and saw some of my teammates waking up from their naps and beginning to prepare mentally for the week ahead. Others were light and excited to be leading the day camp. I finished my drink and began writing in my journal. Twenty minutes later, the plane touched down and we shuffled off to find our bags.

Once we had been reunited with our luggage, we met our leaders for the week: a couple named Rick and Liz Greer. Rick and Liz had moved from Milton, Ontario in 2000 to run Eagle Bay Camp in Hilbre, Manitoba. In 2000, someone from Manitoba had come to their church in Milton and shared with them the stories of the children who lived in Central Manitoba. Moved by what they had heard, they decided to help lead Eagle Bay Camp as it was looking for more staff.

Seven years later, Rick and Liz had a different vision. They wanted to host day camps in the children's villages rather than having the kids leave their homes to go to camp. The summer of 2008 was the first time this vision came to life.

Our team of six entered Rick and Liz's large, white van outside the airport. We drove three and a half hours north to a campground near the village where we would be running the day camp. At the campsite, we met five others from Winnipeg. Of the fourteen team members, I was one of four who had not been to Eagle Bay Camp.

Our team bonded quite quickly. Rick and Liz did a good job of choosing the team and made sure we worked together on simple tasks from the start, like making dinner and setting up tents. By sunset that evening, everyone was beginning to feel comfortable being around each other.

The next day, we took a tour of the village where we would be hosting the day camp. The village was called Little Saskatchewan and it was a First Nations community. In all my travelling, I had never been to such a community, but I was comfortable in the role of minority. As in many of my global experiences, I was part of the minority in Little Saskatchewan. As we toured the village, we were greeted with strange looks from the locals, but that was to be expected as strangers to a remote village.

As we drove around, Rick and Liz told us stories about Little Saskatchewan. They told us about some of the social and political dynamics as well as some of the challenges the local children faced. Little Saskatchewan was not like any neighbourhood I had lived in, nor was it what I expected to see or hear about in Canada.

While I was growing up, all my needs – and more – were catered for. My parents wanted the best for me and my brother; they made sure we were given support for school and sports, while encouraging us to be the best we could, whatever it was that we decided to put our hands to. I grew up in an upper middle-class neighbourhood and close to our house lived some of the wealthiest people in Canada.

By age six, I would walk with my older brother to school without any parental supervision. We enjoyed three meals a day, snacks, new shoes and clothes for every season. We lived in a temperature, regulated home that gave us relief from the hottest and coldest of days. For the most part, I thought most Canadians lived liked my family did.

As I drove through Little Saskatchewan with Rick and Liz, my picture of Canada was being distorted.

During the week of camp, I was struck by more images and stories of Little Saskatchewan – the symptoms of a broken society. The face of an eight-year-old boy was chubby, but not a chubbiness caused by obesity. I had seen children in Rwanda with the same features. The Little Saskatchewan boy was malnourished. I tried to comprehend how a child living in Canada could be suffering from malnutrition like a child in Rwanda. Regardless of how, the injustice seared itself on my mind the same way. And there was more. There were pregnant teenagers, substance abuse and a failing education system. The more I saw, the heavier my heart became. I pictured the children going home at night and enduring these difficulties and more.

Each day at the camp, a co-leader and I had a discussion time with kids aged ten to thirteen, in an attempt to get them to open up about their lives. We decided to focus one particular discussion on hopes and dreams for the future. We asked the kids various questions and even talked about what hopes and dreams we had when we were growing up, but the kids were silent. We finally asked them point blank: "Don't you have any hopes and dreams?"

One of the most influential girls in the group spoke up, "Why would we have any hopes or dreams about our lives? What we have and what's around us is all there is. There is nothing more."

The words were likes echoes from Rwanda.

That night our team sat down with Rick and Liz to discuss how things at the day camp were going. We talked about highlights and challenges. We spoke about the lives of the children and shared some of the stories the children told us about their lives.

Our team began to ask Rick and Liz big questions. We asked about why certain things existed in the community, such as neglect, abuse and mismanagement. Having led many weeks of camp in Central Manitoba, Liz knew that these questions would come. She had prepared a presentation to try to help those who had questions understand the context of the world we were a part of in Little Saskatchewan.

Liz talked to us about the history of First Nations in Canada and reminded us of things we vaguely remembered learning in school or saw on television. She talked about the last 200 years, which saw First Nations discriminated against, banished to reserves and forced to suffer through the residential school system that fractured countless societies. The more Liz spoke, the more the voices of the children I had met that week got louder. My mind travelled to Rwanda again.

I travelled to Rwanda in November of 2005. The purpose of the trip was to meet young church leaders and hear how they were bringing the voice of love and truth to their community. The trip was also an opportunity to learn about the nationwide genocide that happened in 1994, which saw over 800,000 people killed in 100 days.

One of the trips I took in Rwanda was to a genocide memorial centre in Kigali, Rwanda's capital. When I arrived there, my travelling companions and I were welcomed by two military officers, who graced us with smiles. They ushered us into the classroom-sized building. On the walls, there were quotes and pictures of the Rwandan genocide.

As I looked around the room, I discovered one section of the memorial centre that was dedicated to other genocides. It was a large plaque that listed genocides in other countries during the last 500 years. I saw the Jewish Holocaust of World War Two, the genocide in the former Yugoslavia and then one that baffled me. On the list was the genocide that occurred in North America. I needed a moment to remember what had happened from 1500 to 1970 in North America. When I remembered, I thought to myself, *a genocide was not how my text books and teachers described it*. But what had happened in North America to Aboriginals was an atrocity, and I was thankful that the Rwandans recognized just how destructive it was. For almost 500 years in Canada, Aboriginal people suffered through injustice.

Back in the gymnasium in Little Saskatchewan, my mind began to race. I realized how poor my history education was. I felt embarrassed and angry as a Canadian. My education had failed me. My country had failed our beloved Aboriginal people.

After coming to these conclusions, I asked myself, "Were we continuing to fail our Aboriginal people?"

When I returned to the campsite that night, I was feeling sick with what I now knew. I remained quiet while getting ready for bed; deep in thought, I kneeled and prayed before getting into my sleeping bag as images of Little Saskatchewan and its children – along with images of Aboriginals from past generations – flashed through my mind. As I prayed, I began to cry uncontrollably. Generation upon generation of pain and misery, for so long, hidden from my sight, were now placed in front of me. I could not look away.

When our team returned to the school the next morning to lead the day camp, we had renewed energy. We were focused and more sensitive to the needs of the children. We worked in unity as a team. The children seemed in tune with us, too. The days that followed went extremely well, and by the end of the week, we had forged a bond with the children.

Although Rick and Liz were impressed with how our team served the children, I could not shake the darker images of Little Saskatchewan. The children's stories and the history lesson latched onto me. I was thankful for my experience and for each person I met, but I felt unsettled. That Canada could allow any of its citizens to live like this did not seem real.

Growing up, my picture of Canada was pristine. Living in my parents' home shaped my perspective, but so did my education and travels. At each level of school, I received encouragement and discipline. My teachers believed in my abilities and wanted me to achieve academically what they thought I was capable of.

The student body at my middle school was a rainbow of human colours. There were children from every continent and ethnicity. In my elementary school, staff and students would have an annual celebration of culture called Caravan. Kids from class would wear clothing from their native country, bring traditional food and show us things from their culture, including art and dance.

During the warmer months, I got to play games and have fun with friends at recess and lunch time. We ran through the fields and around the baseball diamond. We laughed, climbed monkey bars and traded hockey cards. I was happy at home and happy at school.

When I travelled throughout Canada, I saw the Pacific and Atlantic coasts. I looked across the majestic Rockies and neon blue glacier streams. I heard the French language and the Maritime fiddles. I felt the coolness of the great lakes in Ontario and the hardness of the red clay in Prince Edward Island. I believed Canada to be a land of beauty and a place of equality.

On the return flight from Winnipeg, I questioned my childhood picture. The anger and embarrassment were growing in me. There was an unspoken rage building as I retreated in long runs and night walks to contemplate what I had seen.

Within two months of my trip, the cares and worries of everyday life had caught up with me. I did not forget the children of Little Saskatchewan, but they were no longer in the forefront of my mind. In October of 2008, Rick and Liz came to Mississauga for a visit. They were giving presentations about the work they had done with their day camps in six First Nations communities in Central Manitoba. I sat with about three dozen other members of my church in a large home while Rick and Liz spoke about their work. When they showed pictures of the children, the emotions I had when I was in Little Saskatchewan resurfaced. The stories they told about children from other communities were like the stories of the children of Little Saskatchewan. Part of me wanted to leave and take a long drive to vent.

At the end of the presentation, Rick came over to me. He had no idea what I was feeling. He asked me how I was, then proposed an idea.

"Bryce, how would you like to join us in Manitoba for a winter road trip?" he asked.

"What is a winter road trip?" I said.

"Well, it is a week-long tour of three First Nations communities during the winter in which a team would lead gym days and gym nights."

Still wrestling with my emotions, I responded: "Okay, but why is it is called a winter road trip?"

"Because the roads we travel on are winter roads." Rick paused and then before I could ask him another question, he continued: "Winter roads are frozen lakes and rivers. Don't worry. The ice is four to five feet thick. Even transport trucks drive on them."

I had cooled down by the end of the conversation. Initially, I was hesitant about travelling on frozen lakes and rivers, but the idea of returning to Manitoba was appealing. The opportunity would give me a healthy outlet for my anger. Instead of suppressing it or lashing out on some innocent person, I could help Rick and Liz, and more importantly, give a day of fun to kids who don't always get it. I also knew that the more time I could spend with these children, the better I would be able to share their story if and when the time came.

On a cold February morning in 2009, I boarded another plane heading for Winnipeg. Accompanying me on the plane, was my close friend, Zaya, and two young adults from my church, Jason and Nick.

Rick and Liz picked us up at the airport and were enthusiastic about our energetic and athletic team. Before we left, Zaya had the privilege of speaking with the former leader of the Liberal Party of Canada, Michael Ignatieff. Being a political science major, Zaya could not pass up the opportunity when he saw Mr. Ignatieff sitting alone in the airport food court. Zaya wished him all the best of luck going forward. Mr. Ignatieff then told Zaya that he thought what he was doing in Manitoba was admirable and truly Canadian. Zaya humbly thanked him.

We packed all of our gear into a trailer hitched to Rick and Liz's van. Before leaving the city, we needed to pick up one more team member: Michelle. She was a university student from Winnipeg and had worked with Rick and Liz many times before. Michelle might have had the most difficult task of the team, having to put up with four young men, but she was confident she could hold her own.

We drove two and a half hours north to Rick and Liz's home on the first day. We would spend the night there. Their home was a lovely setting for our team's preparation and would also be a place of luxury compared to our other accommodations. Most of our week would be spent in either the van or a gym.

After a delicious home-cooked meal, our team retired to the living room to discuss the week. We were well prepared for what we were going to see. In the communities we would visit, dropping out of high school, teenage pregnancy, neglect, substance abuse and domestic violence were commonplace – in fact, they happened four times as often than elsewhere in Canada.

Rick told us that we were not going to fix any child's situation with one gym night or gym day, but what we could do was, "let them feel like a kid for a day", which became our motto for the trip.

We were unified in our desire to serve the kids with every ounce of energy we had. We were not their saviours, but we could all play an important role for a day and give them some hope for the days ahead.

The sun rose brightly on the powder snow of Manitoba. The day was calm and minus 25 degrees in the morning, our nostrils sticking from the cold as we re-packed all of our gear into the trailer. Our first destination on the winter road tour was Bloodvein. The drive was two and a half hours of which twenty minutes was spent driving across Lake Winnipeg.

The four of us from the Toronto area were still a little uncomfortable about crossing the lake. I had never done anything like this and was scolded by my parents as a child if I ever neared a frozen lake. We pulled up to a warning sign located where the shore of Lake Winnipeg was. We all hopped out of the van like tourists and took pictures. When we re-entered the van, we took a collective deep breath and Rick drove the van over the lake, and twenty minutes later we emerged, shaken but unscathed.

The experience of driving on winter roads was a truly Canadian encounter. However, what we were going to witness on the reserves was not a typical Canadian occurrence, nor would it sit well with any of us. What we would see was something that a high school student from my church described as "a little bit of Africa in Canada."

If you asked me about child poverty in Canada before 2008, I would have said three things: it was predominantly found in urban centres; it was in broken or single parent families; such poverty would result in children not receiving multiple gifts at Christmas.

I never would have imagined children without clean drinking water, children unable to afford healthy food or children who did not have hope, dreams or imagination. The poverty I saw in 2008 in Little Saskatchewan was a debilitating poverty. It was systematic and cyclical, and it greatly affected the mind and spirit of the children. What we witnessed on the three isolated communities in Central Manitoba that week was even more astounding.

In each reserve, we led a gym night in school gymnasiums. Before the gym programs, we had about two hours to set up and have a light lunch late in the afternoon. When we set up the gym for the kids, we would walk around the schools. In two of the three schools, the taps in the washrooms did not work. If the taps did work, the water was not drinkable. In two of the gymnasiums, the physical education equipment was far below the standards of a typical Canadian school. It was the same with the textbooks in the classrooms.

I remember when I was a boy in school, I loved going to gym class. There was always plenty of variety in the activities we got to do. When we were given a break by our teacher, the class would race out to the water fountains. In class, we had textbooks in good condition and a library filled with books. How could the schools from my childhood and the ones I visited in Central Manitoba exist in the same country?

On the last night of the winter road tour, our team hosted a gym night at Bloodvien Reserve. Rick and Liz invited all the youth to join us for two hours of volleyball, basketball and floor hockey. It was important to involve the youth in the programming.

In the reserves we had visited, none of the reserves provided high school education past grade ten and two of the three reserve schools only offered classes up to grade eight. In order for youth to complete their high school diploma, they had to travel south and live away from home and their families. Half the youth would fail or drop out. This meant that many of the teens that we met at the gym night on Bloodvien reserve had dropped out of school. There was very little for them to do, especially in the winter. So in a simple and practical way we were offering them a night of fun and relaxation. It was a time that gave them a feeling of belonging and experience the beauty of being a child. The gym night was going well. We managed to clearly communicate to the younger children that it was the older kids' turn to have fun. The young boys and girls watched or played jump rope on the sidelines.

Halfway through the night a little girl came into the gym. I had seen her at the gym earlier in the week. She said something to her older brother, at which point they both left. However, several minutes later, their teenage sister joined the volleyball game, followed by her little sister, who had returned without her brother.

"Where did your brother go?" I asked the little girl.

"He had to go home because our baby sister is at home and our mom is too drunk to take care of her. My older sister was taking care of her in the first hour, and now it is my older brother's turn."

There were many moments like this one that stung. One girl told us her six-year-old brother just started smoking. We saw another little girl without a hat and mittens because her parents could not afford them. We also saw a seven-year-old boy walking home after a gym night by himself when it was minus 30 degrees outside. His home was over half an hour away from the school.

When I was a child, I remember singing "O Canada" with such pride and enthusiasm because of how great a country I believed Canada was. When I reached middle school, we heard different renditions of the anthem each morning. One morning would be a traditional rendition with a choir, the next a more modern version with an R&B group singing "O Canada" A Cappella. We would also hear the anthem in both official languages.

Hearing "O Canada" each morning made you believe in your country more. I even had a favourite part of the song. To me, it was the line in the song that I believed to be the truest. I would sing even more patriotically when I sang, "God keep our land glorious and free." I believed that our country was glorious and free, and I believed that because of the way I lived. In my parents' home, at my school and when I travelled, I believed those words were not just a prayer, but also a reminder for Canadians to respond daily to those in our country who were struggling and governed by misfortune. I truly believed that Canadians wanted every other Canadian to be glorious and free. The words were a promise.

But while I stood in Bloodvein's school gym I felt the promise had been broken. I began to think that the prayer was only said with self-interest so that individuals' families and friends would have abundance, but not the whole country. As I stood in the gym, I felt as if the Canadian flag had been pulled over my eyes my whole life. Our nation was not "glorious and free" – not when we had thousands of Canadian children living in Third World conditions.

CHAPTER TWO: Go Fast or Go Far

WHEN I RETURNED HOME FROM MY SECOND visit to Manitoba, I wanted a microphone in which to tell everyone what was happening to our country. I wanted to yell from the rooftops that our national anthem was a lie. I wanted to challenge the leaders at city halls and on Parliament Hill to begin prioritizing the needs of children over the wants of adults. I was filled with rage, and I was ready to pick a fight with the people I thought were responsible for misdirecting Canadians. Unlike the first time I came back from Manitoba, my tongue was not tied. I knew what I wanted to communicate and articulate. But something within me slowed me down. Something in me knew I would regret my message if it was harsh and hateful. Something in me gave me patience and kept my negativity and judgement silent.

At the end of the same month, the leaders of my church invited a bishop from Kenya to speak to the congregation. Since my trip to Rwanda, I was always keen to meet and listen to someone from the Great Lakes District of Africa. Despite my inner hostility, I was eager to understand any hope they had for the future.

The bishop started his speech by greeting the congregation on behalf of his church in Kenya. He also introduced us to his son Paul who thanked our church for our kind reception. The bishop then returned to the microphone:

"I want to begin my message with a Kenyan proverb, 'If you want to go fast, go alone. If you want to go far, go together.'"

Everything around me stopped. It was an odd feeling for me as a pastor not to be focused on those around me, but for the next hour I was totally enveloped with the Kenyan proverb. The meaning, humility and wisdom of its words received all of my attention and imagination.

From that day on, I began to see things differently. The anger that once dominated me and raced through my veins, slowed down and began to fade entirely. I was much less interested in pointing out the greed of others. I no longer wanted to call out and blame Canadian leaders who were acting irresponsibly. My focus turned to the needs of the children I had met in Manitoba. It all happened so quickly, but somehow the proverb had turned off the detonator of negativity inside me.

Words from another wise man also came to me as my desire to blame decreased and my want to find a solution increased:

"These problems don't take seconds to solve,
and getting' mad ain't the same thing as getting involved.
We need to get up even if they knock us down.
They can't stop us.
Smile right back at 'em laugh and then get up.
Actions speak louder than a thousand talkers,
so make 'em blast that in their walkmans."

– Shad K

By the summer of 2009, I began to brainstorm. In my community, I began advocating weekly for the children I had met. My church was now sending two teams a year to help Rick and Liz, and we were also building a partnership with another reserve in London that was going through similar difficulties as the communities in Central Manitoba.

My brainstorming, however, was nationally focused. I wanted to tell the story of Amy and the children on the reserves in Central Manitoba to the entire country. I wanted to make it an awareness campaign in the ways that I was gifted. It was a thought, but I was not sure how that would practically come together. Another idea was to tug on the educators of the provinces to tell the full story of the aboriginal people, including their current place in Canadian society. A third idea was to build a network of like-minded people and share stories and resources to stoke youth groups and classrooms into action. Ideas came and went. I knew there were already people working night and day on the cause too, and I did not want to reinvent an idea. So I continued to listen, brainstorm and advocate in my church community. That was until September of the same year.

When I had returned from Manitoba the second time, my anger was producing ideas that accused and judged people in Canada. I saw wealth near to me, and I immediately and unfairly concluded that these people were selfish and needed to change. When I thought of ways I could get those near to me to help the children in Central Manitoba, I thought of messages that would produce guilt. It was not a healthy message or method, and I am glad I did not speak to people that way. Out of my anger, I also saw people as apathetic or ignorant. But with the Kenyan proverb running through my mind, my perspective of Canadians was being restored, and a new idea emerged that was much more positive.

In September 2009, my brainstorming centred on encouraging Canadians to be involved in renewing the lives of young Canadians. I wanted to encourage people to participate by bringing to the forefront the beauty and joy of the children. I knew this would make a lasting difference. When I visited the children, this is what won me over too. I saw their difficulties, but I also heard their laughter and innocence. Even in their sickness, loneliness and hurt, I saw the beauty and joy of the children. It is the light that shines that overcomes the darkness, no matter how small the light.

I wanted to tell stories about the enduring and resilient nature of the children. I wanted to show Canadians their strength. In hearing about the children of Central Manitoba, I believed my fellow Canadians would be generous in building something positive for these kids. If I could tell the children's story and reveal their wonderful nature, I knew positive actions would follow. I wanted people to not just give money, but build lasting partnerships that brought awareness and hope. I also did not want to be a lone voice; I wanted to connect Canadians to each other and allow them to be the change.

At the end of work days, I spent many hours in solitude walking and running – sometimes for two hours a day. People have called me a running monk because I run long distances by myself, usually without music while reflecting about important decisions or conversations.

During the last weekend of the month, I travelled with a friend to a cottage in Muskoka, Ontario. The space was as calm as the placid water next to the cottage. It gave me the right environment for listening. I ate simply and listened deeply for the two days at the cottage.

And then on Saturday evening it came.

I would run.

The idea of running across Canada – the second biggest country in the world – was a massive feat. I was not Terry Fox, but I knew there was something attractive to the Canadian heart when someone journeyed from coast to coast on foot, and it was something that Canadians – including the children – would support me throughout my endeavours. Most importantly, a run across Canada would help me raise awareness about the many children living in poverty in our country – children like those in Little Saskatchewan.

After I shared the idea with a friend, we talked about what it might be like to cross Canada. We talked about people's reactions and best and worst case scenarios. I dreamed aloud and tried to celebrate the moment. I had spent a lot of time seeking the right answer and getting my heart in the right place. I slept well that night.

The next morning my mind and heart were buzzing with the idea of crossing Canada. The training for this run would be more intense than anything I had ever trained for. It would need my full attention.

There was, however, something that lingered from my friend's initial response that I had to consider. When would I be able to run across Canada? If I ran the same distance as Terry Fox – 42 kilometres a day (the equivalent of a marathon) – I would finish the trek in eight to ten months. This length of time included a margin for days off due to possible injuries and other setbacks.

Another question came to my mind: "If I am going to run across Canada, would I have to leave my job?" A floodgate was opened. Crossing Canada sounded like a good idea, but was it possible?

At this point in the story, I am sure you are asking yourself many questions about my idea to run across Canada. Here are my answers to the three I received the most often after I told people about my plan:

Q: At that time, could I run long distances?

A: Yes. I had been running between 30 to 90 kilometres a week from 1997 until 2007. In 2007, I trained for and ran my first marathon. In 2008, I ran my second marathon, which happened to be the Boston Marathon. I then ran a half marathon in the spring of 2009.

Q: Why choose to run across Canada?

I enjoy running and the decision to run across Canada also worked as a slow method of transportation. Ultimately, the journey would be slow and therefore I would be able to talk to people in each city and even invite them to join me on the run.

Q: What is one major advantage of running across Canada over biking or driving across Canada?

A major advantage of running across Canada is the reaction from people who are amazed that you would do it. Running would interest more people than any other cross-Canada trip, and such curiosity would enable me to share my motivation.

All these questions aside, what I had was only an idea. What would it take for this idea to come to life?

For some Canadians, the reality these children live in left a sour taste in their mouths. "How can Canada have children living like this?" Others would respond, "Well, the parents are probably not working hard enough, and it is their fault their kids are in the situation they are in."

In talking with Rick and Liz about how families could be in such lowly economic positions, they explained there are many factors involved. However, Rick said something to our winter road trip team in 2009 that stuck with me: "No matter what the parents have done, or not done, and no matter whose mistakes have created the impoverished state for the families or the communities, the poverty is not the fault of the children. Being poor is never the kids' fault."

I repeated these words to many people I spoke to and would add, "You can point the finger at adults all you want, saying they are to blame, but it will not help the children. The kids never chose to be living in such vulnerable conditions and, until there are Canadians willing to partner with these communities, the cycle of poverty is unlikely to break."

I would think about the children often over the next four months. During this time, I intentionally had dinners with Zaya, Nick and Jason to discuss our winter road trip. All three guys had distinct personalities and perspectives. Jason and Nick were two sharp students with giant hearts for children. They thought very critically about the problems the children faced and how they could elevate the children's story in their discussions with peers. They also gave me a window into what the younger generation of adults were thinking and how important it was to talk about injustices happening in Canada. Their friendship and opinions were valuable to me as I reflected on the trip we took and my advocacy going forward.

Zaya was a good friend who I had met four years prior. Our relationship began through shared interests like sports and politics, but we formed a brotherhood out of deep love for people. Zaya was vital during the fall of 2009 as I processed my advocacy, because he would challenge me to think about the opposing arguments and opinions that others might have. He also held me accountable to make sure I kept my word and stood by my convictions.

My conversations with Jason, Nick and Zaya were encouraging, however, exhausting, as we had a tendency to stay up well past our bedtimes. Nevertheless, my three friends kept me focused.

The children were constantly on my mind, and although their struggle was heavy on my heart, I was not burdened. In fact, when I thought of the children, I would experience joy, thinking about how resilient they were and how much they could laugh, despite the hardship they faced. I also had no guilt for not being with them. When I left Central Manitoba, the children never told me I was betraying them for leaving, they just hoped I would return. They wanted me and others from our teams to return because they had made friends with us and wanted to see us again. And so I returned, actively waiting for the right time to run across Canada with their story.

CHAPTER THREE:
Twists and Turns

IN LIFE AND IN RUNNING, TIMING IS EVERY-
thing. Depending on the timing of an encounter, its outcome can
be completely different. I went to Paris when I was nine years old;
the city meant nothing to me. However, during the same year, I
watched a movie called *Cry Freedom*, and because of who I was,
at that time, the movie had a significant impact on my life. When
the timing is right, a simple message can alter a person's trajec-
tory completely – like billiard balls colliding on a table. When I
met the children of Little Saskatchewan, the timing was right; I
had the confidence to tell their story and to challenge people to
make a positive difference. When the idea came to run across the
country, however, I was uncertain of the timing.

In 2009, I was married to a woman I loved and had a job that
mattered deeply to me. In order to run across Canada, I would
need time, resources and support. With a job of great responsi-
bility, like being a pastor, and to be married – something which
requires both people to be together and be supportive for it to
be optimal – the thought of running across Canada felt too com-
plicated. I asked God for insight, but nothing came until my life
changed.

The fall of 2009 was a very dark and stressful time for me.
Communication broke down between my wife and I, and our

marriage dissolved. I felt as low as I ever had. I was angry, resentful and sad. My worst nightmare was now in living colour. I would not wish divorce on my worst enemy.

In dark and low moments, I believe it is essential for every person to have a good community or circle of friends and family around them. Even the most ordinary stresses and confusions require friends and loved ones to be present. When darkness ambushed me, and negative thoughts and emotions invaded, I was so fortunate to be in a great community and to have wonderfully supportive friends and family.

As a pastor, I thought my job was in jeopardy when my marriage ended. There is a lot expected of pastors – sometimes to be near perfect or have super human resistance to bad things happening to them. When the marriage first unravelled, I was tight lipped, not wanting people to doubt my leadership or faith. Then I realized the façade of perfection was truly a lie as God is most powerful when we are honest and admit our mistakes, or when we show our need for God in times of weakness.

I began telling people in my church and even the youth and young adults who I pastored about what had happened. I trusted in God and in my community, and because of that trust, I found great strength in my weakness and light in the darkness. By the spring of 2010, the dream and idea of running across Canada resurfaced, and there was peace in my heart that the timing of the run was not far away. When I look back, I am still surprised how quickly I began to plan for the run after such a heartbreaking event. In some respects, the project helped me heal and not be overcome by the sadness.

When the idea of running across Canada came to me, my thoughts were almost entirely practical. How am I going to cross Canada in five or six months by myself? Do I want to be on the road for ten months?

I came to the conclusion that I did not want to be on the road for ten months, although I knew that there was no way I could finish a cross-Canada run in five to six months on my own. So, I asked myself a critical question: Would the run and its message be more powerful if I ran with others?

When I first heard the Kenyan proverb, I came face to face with my own limitations. I could not end child poverty by myself. I knew I would have to work with people who were already working at this goal. I realized the run and its message would go farther if I ran with a team. I also felt that there would be a greater attraction for youth and children if they saw a team running rather than just an individual. Each person would bring a slightly different perspective and motivation to the run. By having a team, maybe kids would see themselves more able to be involved.

But if I was going to run with a team, who would they be? And how would the run function? In the spring of 2010, I went on many long walks, brainstorming ideas. I had long discussions in pubs and cafes, using my friends as sounding boards. I reflected back to my childhood, to the two runs that had the greatest impact on my life: Terry Fox's Marathon of Hope and the Olympic Torch relay. I wanted to bring the best of these runs together – a relay that would fight for the cause and create unity all at once.

I wanted to run far.

I took the idea to a few of my friends and my parents – yes, even at 32 years old, I respected and appreciated the advice of my parents. I hope I never lose that. Everyone had questions and constructive criticism. I would modify my idea and present it, again, to another friend. Everyone thought it was great, but a wee bit idealist. Not a surprising response when it comes to me. I felt the time had arrived for me to take the idea forward to others and begin to build the team.

The first team member I was looking for was a humanitarian organization to support the run. My talents were boldness, running and speaking. But I needed expertise and someone to promote the cause to Canadians. I was not famous. If a stranger found out that Bryce Dymond was going to be running across Canada, it would probably not shift a stranger's life – even in a small way – to get involved. However, if I could get a well-known and well-respected humanitarian organization behind me, it might grab people's attention.

In a very short time, I made a short list of Canadian humanitarian organizations that I wanted to support the run. The two finalists were World Vision and Free the Children. I had a lot of respect for both, but at first Free the Children was the front runner. They are incredible at engaging young people and empowering them to see the problems in the world and seek to embody the positive change needed. I felt strongly that our message needed to be heard by youth, first and foremost. It would be the next generation that would bring about the greatest change in their lives.

World Vision Canada also had a tremendous reputation, however, it happened to be the organization that my mom volunteered for as chair of the board. My mom proudly waves the flag of the organization and therefore I acknowledged the guilt I would feel if I chose Free the Children.

When I spoke to my mom about my short list, she of course thought World Vision was the best choice. "Talk to World Vision first, and if they are not interested, then go to Free the Children," she said. I did not feel any pressure from my mom and was glad to receive her blessing if I did end up partnering with Free the Children.

I began writing drafts of proposals I would present. It was not something I was naturally good at, but I knew it had to be done. The proposal would give World Vision the chance to see that I had a well-thought-out project – and one that would benefit them too. This was important because a large organization like World Vision receives countless ideas and they can't say yes to everyone. They have to make the best decision for their organization based on whether or not the project shares their values.

When I finished the proposal, I sent it directly via email to Dave Toycen, the President of World Vision Canada. Mr. Toycen is a personal friend of my mother. Within two weeks, Mr. Toycen had responded to me and arranged for me to meet with a couple employees who support volunteer initiatives. I was nervous to go to the meeting, feeling that my idea would be seen as too difficult to implement. I also knew that World Vision focused most of their efforts overseas, and the idea of them supporting a project focused on children in Canada might not be in line with their values and plans.

I presented my proposal to World Vision, and to my surprise, the organization's representatives responded enthusiastically:

"Bryce, this proposal is exciting. Over the last five years, our organization has been doing a ton of research on child poverty in Canada. Although our focus is mainly on children in the developing world, some Canadian children live in developing world conditions, and we have started to make partnerships with smaller Canadian organizations that share World Vision's values. Your run might be just the kind of event that would ignite our national work and help provide some much-needed funding."

I was bouncing on the inside.

At the end of the meeting, I shook hands with the two World Vision employees, and they said they would get back to me in a couple of weeks. And they did! In May, World Vision accepted the proposal.

With the support of World Vision, I now knew the run was going to happen. World Vision would handle the promotion and provide media relations for the project. The next recruiting task was to find people crazy enough to travel and run with me.

I first thought of my community and my closest friends and family. The first two people I asked were my good friend Zaya and my father, because I felt strongly that they would be my best teammates.

Zaya and I went on many trips together, including the trip to Central Manitoba. He understood and supported the mission of the run. Zaya also knew me well, and understood what I felt in my heart. We had supported each other in difficult times and I knew he was the right choice; however, if for some reason he could not come with me, I knew he would support me throughout my endeavours. Nevertheless, I could think of no other person that I would want with me on the road.

Zaya also had the determination, physique and athleticism to run long distances. He and I had ran a half marathon together, and we had played in dozens of basketball and soccer matches. He had endurance and pace and would do the hard work of training to perform at his best if he committed to the run.

Months before World Vision approved the proposal, my dad agreed to drive the support vehicle. Throughout my life, my dad was heavily involved in my athletic activities and coached and played sports on his own. He enjoyed running and the camaraderie of a team. In his retirement, my dad helped organize projects and recruit volunteers. In many ways, his example gave me a model to organize the run.

In the early stages of the summer, both Zaya and my dad agreed to be part of the team. I knew I would have to recruit more, but they were a good starting point. Zaya said he would join me for not just part, but all of my run. This was a massive announcement and huge boost of confidence. My dad committed to being with the team for the month of June and would travel to the finish line in Vancouver with my mom at the end of September.

Still, there was one team member that I needed to recruit. The person needed qualities and talents that Zaya and I did not have. It took the whole summer for that person to emerge, but when she did, I was elated to invite her aboard.

Brittany was a young adult at the church in Mississauga where I was pastor. She was gifted in administration and had travelled to several poor communities in Canada and in the Dominican Republic. She worked as a live-in nanny and was studying early child education at university. Her heart was centred on children, and she had a passion for vulnerable children. Brittany would bring balance with her gifts and skills but also with her personality. She was far more structured and task orientated than Zaya and I and had the roar of a *Mama Bear*, which would be needed to keep us focused on the priorities and schedule of the run.

In September 2010, the team was assembled; World Vision, Brittany, Zaya and I would be running across Canada to raise awareness about the one in ten Canadian children who lived in poverty. Our run would raise funds for local Canadian organizations that partnered with World Vision. My dad and fourteen others signed up to travel with the team for a week or two at a time to help with driving and running.

The actual travel time for the run would be five and a half months. The team would leave in late April from Toronto, arrive in St. John's four days later, beginning the run on May 1, 2011. For the next five months, we would make our way to the Pacific shores of Vancouver. The goal was to run 70 kilometres a day, six days a week. We called our run the One Nation Run, a name suggested by a World Vision employee. Our goal was twofold: first, to tell one hundred thousand Canadians, through speaking engagements and media, that there was hundreds of thousands of children living in conditions of global poverty in Canada, and second, to raise a toonie for every person who heard about the run. We had seven months to get ready.

* * *

At the end of June, I ended my time as pastor to youth and young adults at Lorne Park Baptist Church. It was a decision I knew I had to make, but a tough one because of my relationships with the leaders and students I worked with. I then took three months to travel, reflect and be with close friends in the summer to process my divorce so that I could be ready for the One Nation Run. By the end of the summer, I felt like I was on solid ground and ready to move forward in life and with the run. And then I was blindsided.

At the end of the summer, two close friends were getting married. They had asked me to stand beside them as a witness to their marriage and be in their wedding party. Over a hundred people attended the wedding, including a young lady named Catherine, who I was partnered with and together we happened to walk down the aisle. Initially, I was curious — she was the only person I did not know in the wedding party. I had heard a great deal about her through the bride and groom, but we had never crossed paths until the wedding. After meeting her, I became more intrigued. She was grounded in family and faith, and as LL Cool J would say, she "was an around the way girl", meaning down to earth, easy on the eyes and confident in who she was.

I watched how Catherine acted around people; it was evident that people and especially her friends mattered to her. After the wedding, I talked to her and asked if I could visit her the following weekend. We hit it off, and within two months of dating, I needed to further my investigation; in November, I moved to Ottawa.

It was an unexpected turn of events. Romance was not something that I had been looking for, yet something had happened to me the day I met Catherine. She had altered my life, and more so, I now had another teammate for the One Nation Run.

CHAPTER FOUR: Cold Calls

IT WAS 9:00 A.M. MY RUNNING GEAR WAS ON, AND I was warmed up. I needed to be prepared as I was about to run 30 kilometres. I also needed to be warm as it was negative 23 degrees Celsius with a wind chill. I was excited and a little nervous. The last time I ran 30 kilometres was in the spring of 2008 when I ran a marathon. Since that time, I had run over twenty kilometres a dozen or so times. This would be the longest run I had done in such a cold temperature, yet something I was not looking forward to.

In January of 2011, I was less than four months away from being in St. John's. The clock on the project was spinning, and there was still so much to do. One Nation Run had a promotional video, posters and an official website. But there were still churches to call and runners to recruit in every town and province.

The plan for the run was to travel 70 kilometres a day before the Rockies, and then 60 kilometres in the Rockies, as I guessed that would be the most challenging section of the run. Zaya committed to running ten kilometres; I planned to run 21, and we talked Brittany into running two kilometres. We thought Brittany would feel lazy or left out if she was the only person on the team not running. Brittany was not thrilled about the idea of running, but she thanked us later after many delicious desserts were presented to us by our hosts. As a team, we had 33 kilometres covered, but the relay still needed to cover another 37 if the One Nation Run was going to arrive in Vancouver on September 30, 2011.

The route was to go through every major town and city in the country, with the exception of Charlottetown, Prince Edward Island. The total distance was approximately 8,700 kilometres. If we were not successful in getting enough runners to participate in the event, then I was confident we could modify our travel plans. I believed, however, that it was possible to recruit local runners for the One Nation Run when we came by their hometown.

I believed my training had to match the intensity of what I would do on the run. Through a rigorous training schedule, I averaged 100 kilometres a week. Along with full body strength and conditioning workouts and stretching routines, my body, and most importantly my legs and lungs, were getting stronger each day. The running was not easy. I ran primarily outdoors facing a mean north wind and dozens of snow storms and squalls. The weather was as unforgiving as the concrete I ran on. Each day of training averaged three hours of exercise, including warm-ups and then cooling down. I burned roughly 1,300 calories a day, and so needed to eat over 3,000 calories a day just to maintain my already lean and narrow frame.

When I wasn't running, stretching or eating, I was calling out to complete strangers from east to west. The vision I had was to be housed by families in each town and city the run ended in. I chose this more grassroots way of finding accommodations despite it being much more laborious. My belief was if people could open their doors and lives to perfect strangers, they could open their doors and lives to those children near to them going through difficult times. Remember, I am an idealist.

Each day, I would spend two hours calling churches in towns and villages in Newfoundland and the Maritimes, hoping someone would either answer my call, return my call or, if I was really lucky, say yes to hosting the team. Most calls I made would be coupled with an email to the same church. After being a pastor, I knew it would take diligence to get any communication from the churches I was contacting. I also wrote emails so that the people getting the information would have something to pass on to boards and committees who oversaw the church's public relations. It was inevitable that someone beside the secretary would be in charge of hospitality.

To convince myself I was not going insane by making cold calls, I diversified my communication. Different community groups would invite me to share the message of the run through speaking engagements and Skype conversations. I spoke to university and high school students, shared my story with churches and did interviews with local media outlets. It gave me hope to speak to Canadians about taking care of Canadian children, and it reminded me how important the message I was carrying was. Often, there were times when I spoke to people, even educated Canadians, who had no clue that there were so many children living in poverty and how vulnerable they were. Most people I spoke to, including the media, were concerned and were willing to spread the news to others.

I did have a life outside of the preparations. I lived in Ottawa for a reason. I would visit Catherine five or six times a week in the evenings. While in Ottawa I lived in Gloucester, an eastern borough of the city. I lived with a fine young couple from the church community I now belonged to. Ryan was the husband and Sara was the wife. Most days Ryan and Sara left for work in the morning, so I could go two or three days at a time without seeing them. When I visited Catherine during the evenings, I would take the number 95 bus along Ottawa's marvellous transit way into the downtown where she lived.

On many occasions, when I walked to Catherine's or went out with her to a restaurant, I saw street people. Living on the street is a hard way to go through life and even harder in the winter. It was not a life I envied. The homeless would take refuge near vents or in store doorways where they could find shelter from the wretched north wind. When they asked for money, I would usually say no, but would ask them how they were. Catherine and I would try to take ten or fifteen minutes when we saw street people to ask them if they were hungry or if they needed any winter clothes. We tried to see each one of them as a person and referred to them as our neighbours.

After these encounters I could not help but wonder what their lives must have been like when they were children. Did they suffer abuse at home? Were their parents addicts? Were they bullied at school? Did they have mental illness? I wanted to know what circumstances got them to where they were.

Then I would take my thoughts one step further and think about how my neighbours' lives could be different. How could 'street living' be prevented? When I thought about those living on the streets in Catherine's neighbourhood, it was not long before I thought about the children I knew in Central Manitoba. As much as I respected and valued each person I met on the street, I wanted more for their lives and if it could be prevented, I wanted to help ensure no more children would have a life of begging on city sidewalks.

In the bleak winter days of early February, snow would cover my feet and blur my vision as I ran. At the same time, doubts about the project crept into my mind. The fundraising started at the beginning of January, and after five weeks, the total had yet to reach $5,000. I was trying to build donor momentum, but with little success.

In addition, I was unable to persuade any automobile companies to lend us a vehicle for the trip. A car was something I knew other cross-Canada charity journeys had been able to attain, and I thought the One Nation Run would get one too. The majority of churches I contacted thought that what I was doing was fantastic, but they were unwilling to commit to supporting the run in any way. Even the denomination I had worked in as a youth pastor for nine years backed out of involvement and substantial promotion. These groups did not support the One Nation Run because they were already focused on other programs and events.

Sometimes I considered my efforts on the phone to be futile, and my heart toward such effort grew cold. I was also feeling lonely as I worked. Day in and day out, I sat at Ryan and Sara's kitchen table by myself. The training runs were the same, facing the extreme cold on my own, with only the sun on clear days to accompany me. I wondered when breakthroughs would come. I asked for guidance from the Creator and remembered God's faithfulness during other bleak seasons of my life. I knew better days were around the corner, but the first six weeks of 2011 felt like a runner's wall in a marathon and I had to fight through it with the same determination.

The sign of better days ahead came on February 17, 2011. The day was unusually warm, and the snow melted rapidly as I ran in the heat of the sun. The melting snow banks made small puddles on the sidewalks and roads. It was the first enjoyable run I had in the New Year – the type of run that if time was not an issue I would have kept going until my legs gave out. I felt like a kid as I ran and splashed through puddles. It was like being on a 30-kilometre splash pad.

In the evening, I went to the bus terminal and picked up Zaya. He was visiting for the weekend, and it was his first visit to Ottawa since I had moved. It was a wonderful reunion and one I needed. We ran for an hour on the Saturday, laughed, watched sports and ate filling meals with Catherine and other friends. Being with Zaya reminded me of the importance of teammates and the powerful impact that the presence of a friend can have.

There were some serious discussions and some One Nation Run planning too. Zaya benefitted from the project discussions because he had been mentally locked in on school work (he would graduate at the end of April), and the discussions were good for me because I was having them with someone other than

Ryan and Sara's dog Selah. There were days when I thought Selah was coming with me on the run.

While Zaya was in Ottawa, we also had the pleasure of texting Brittany, who happened to be in Central Manitoba on a winter road trip – the same one Zaya and I had been on in previous years. Brittany's eyes and heart had been opened. She told us how difficult it was to witness the conditions the children were living in. "You can hear stories a million times, but when you experience it for yourself, it changes you," Brittany text us. It was good for us to read her thoughts and feelings on the matter, and it reconnected us to the children who inspired us to do the run.

* * *

After Zaya left, there were only 65 days until our team drove east to St. John's, Newfoundland. In a month and a half I would return to Mississauga for further preparations for the run with Zaya and Brittany. Before then, however, I had to pound the snowy wet pavement and make more phone calls. One day in March, I made a phone call to Corner Brook, Newfoundland. I was trying to find a church that would be willing to support our run by housing us and maybe even promoting the run in their town. It seemed the Salvation Army had a strong presence in Newfoundland, so that's where I started.

When the phone was answered, I heard the voice of an older gentleman: "Hello Salvation Army church." He sounded warm and happy to receive my call.

"Yes hi, my name is Bryce Dymond, and in May of this year, I will be leading a cross-Canada relay to raise awareness and funds for Canadian children living in poverty with World Vision Canada. I was wondering, when the relay enters Corner Brook, if your church would be willing to house me and my friends for the night? I can send you all the details about the run via email if your church is willing."

There was a pause on the other end of the line and then the gentleman said, "Bryce, any friend of the poor is a friend of ours. We would be honoured to help you."

There was then another pause as I tried to figure out if the gentleman was serious. It was, after all, the first time someone had responded positively and immediately. "Wow! That is amazing. Thank you. I will be sure to send you an email with the details of our relay and what our team would request from a host. Thank you so much."

I was stunned as I hung up the phone. I was so touched by this gentleman's response. "Any friend of the poor is a friend of ours." It was what I had been waiting for and knew would come. The call gave me all the hope I needed to keep making calls, regardless of people's responses. I called and called that month, more than I had done previously. Then commitments came from churches and friends of friends to host us. I had emerged through the wall of the preparation and spring was just about ready to break forth.

The days of winter passed and the spring season charged in. The snow liquefied and the ground was thawing. My attitude was also more hopeful and positive, and my speaking engagements were more frequent. The donations were slowly increasing. I had lots to be optimistic about.

I packed up my belongings at Ryan and Sara's place, and on the second Friday of April, I said farewell to Ottawa. Catherine was sad that I was leaving, as you might imagine. We had spent almost every evening together for five months. When I was leaving, Catherine never once asked me to stay. She was supportive throughout her tears and sniffles at the airport. We would see each other at Easter in two weeks in Toronto, and we had plans to spend the rest of our lives together. In other words, this was just the end of our first chapter as a couple.

When I returned to Mississauga, my schedule was packed. I was only there for two and a half weeks, but every day I was busy with last-minute planning and full training sessions. My parents were fantastic while I was back in their home. They drove me to TV interviews and pushed me to return every phone call from donors, interested companies, World Vision employees and accommodation leads. They even hosted a farewell party at their home, which I think was more for my friends and family to ensure they would be free of my presence for six months than it was about celebrating the run. It was a hectic time, but a productive one, full of celebration and encouragement.

One of my speaking engagements in Mississauga was at World Vision's chapel service. Usually the chapel service was only attended by staff members. However, at this particular chapel, dozens of World Vision volunteers were in attendance as it was volunteer appreciation day at the organization.

I was nervous about this speaking engagement. It was not so much because I was speaking to hundreds of people – I had done that many times in my life – but because I felt like they had put a lot of energy into supporting the run and I wanted to show them their support was going to a quality project and communicator. I was also nervous because the World Vision staff worked so hard in advocating for children in other countries. I was worried that the World Vision staff would not understand why their organization was putting energy, time and money into a project focused on Canadian kids. *Don't Canadian kids have it way better than the children we are advocating for overseas?*, I thought they would say. So prior to the speech, I placed a high demand on myself to perform well and persuade effectively.

When I stepped onto the stage and took my place behind the podium, I looked out to the full conference room and that was when my perspective shifted. No longer was I concerned with how I would perform or what people thought of me and the mission I had come up with. No, my focus was now to tell Amy's story, the one compelling story that burned on my lips for over two years. My passion for Amy and the 700,000 plus Canadian children who were in need of basic essentials consumed me. I spoke slowly, paused when I wanted certain facts to soak into the audience's mind and told them Amy's story with sincerity and conviction. When I had concluded the speech and walked off the stage, I was satisfied that the message was not just given but well received.

I spoke to dozens of people after the chapel service finished. Volunteers and World Vision staff told me that they were surprised that poverty had struck children in Canada so harshly. They thanked me for my efforts and encouraged me and my team to be the best advocates we could be while we were on our mission. Others simply said they would be supporting us in prayer and would help spread the message. I felt a great peace after that day – as if those gathered at the chapel represented the majority of Canadians. They might not be able to house our team, run with us or choose to donate to our cause, but the wellbeing of Canadian children mattered to them and they would help in the ways that they could and look to find those families nearest to them who could use a stronger support system. How the One Nation Run would impact Canada in the long-term I did not know, but I felt that our mission would not be in vain and that we would see Canadians young and old become more in tune with those in need within our borders.

Before our departure on April 26, there was one last thing Zaya, Brittany and I had to do. Our last assignment was to go through media training with a World Vision media relations staff member, Genevieve Barber. World Vision wanted the One Nation Run to represent them well. But more than that, they wanted us to be potent communicators. Genevieve was gracious in her instruction and thorough in preparing us for the toughest of interviewers. She told us we had to accomplish three things in every media interview: first, stress that Canadian child poverty exists and is unacceptable in one of the richest nations in the world; second, explain the One Nation Run, and third, plug the website and inform people about how they can donate on it.

Genevieve branded number three in our minds, saying: "If all else fails, and you get stuck or camera shy, just plug the website and one of your teammates will pick you up." Genevieve did not think that we would be interviewed over a hundred times and that our story would be told by over 130 media outlets, but she sure prepared us for it. For all Genevieve did for us, we were eternally grateful.

At 10:00 a.m. on Tuesday April 26, in a packed-to-the-ceiling Pontiac Montana – given generously by the Karasmanis family from my church – we were on our way, heading east along the 401 to St. John's.

CHAPTER FIVE: Home to Strangers

THERE IS A REASON WHY THE HOSPITALITY of the East Coast is so legendary. It is because the legend is true.

People from Ontario return from the Atlantic region with stories about how incredibly well they were treated by East Coasters. They speak of Newfoundlanders and Maritimers alike, that they have jovial spirits and open doors to those who visit. My trip with the team was my seventeenth visit to the East Coast, although I had never been to Newfoundland. Each time I came back from the Atlantic Region, I had hour-long stories about the hospitality of the people.

My visit to Newfoundland was filled with a great anticipation that was shared by Zaya and Brittany. Brittany had been to Newfoundland before, and she was as animated as the rest of us. In our excitement, we all tried to speak with the local accent, although none of us were even close to the real thing. We travelled by ferry across the Maritime waters, for about six hours. The sea sickness we experienced on the vessel briefly muzzled our elation; however, after many laughs and a couple of movies to distract us, the ferry landed at Port-Au-Basques. Our stop for the night was Corner Brook, a two-hour drive away.

Life in Newfoundland is hard. It is the most isolated province in the country. The weather is rough, with high winds that can change the local climate within minutes. The ground is rocky and quite challenging to farm. The once booming fishing industry has been reduced to a shadow of its former self, hamstringing commercial ocean fishing. This meant that many young people after secondary school would travel west to attend school or look for work. Like Irish and Jamaican citizens, there are more Newfoundlanders off the island than on it. Yet through their difficulties, their resilience has solidified. And Newfoundlanders' kindness and respect for each person they encounter has made them famous to everyone who visits.

There were seven of us as a team when we arrived at Corner Brook, with two vehicles as a convoy in the One Nation Run. One vehicle held, Zaya, Brittany, Adam, who was Brittany's boyfriend of four years, and myself. The other was a family station wagon, driven by the McCoy family. The McCoys were friends from Toronto from the very first church I worked at. When Julie McCoy found out that the One Nation Run was recruiting runners for the relay, she sent me an email asking if her husband Tim and oldest daughter Daphne could join us. How could I say no? I loved the McCoy family, and with their participation, we would have all 70 kilometres covered for our relay for the first six days of the One Nation Run. It was a great way to begin the run.

Our convoy stopped at the Corner Brook Salvation Army Church building. The church would be our hosts for this night and one night a week later during the run. We quickly jumped out of the vehicles and entered the building to avoid getting soaked. Once in the lobby we met the pastor Major Calvin Fudge. Major Fudge was a kind man and greeted us graciously. It was a pleasure to meet him in person after speaking on the phone a few weeks prior. Major Fudge introduced himself to the whole team and then introduced other members of the congregation, who arrived just after we had. The four members were there along with the major because they were our hosts for the night. The McCoys would go to the major's home while the rest of us went to four separate homes. The church wanted to make our team feel special by having us in our own home.

It was a cold, wet night in Newfoundland. I was welcomed into the home of a lovely couple named Dave and Carol. When I entered their home, I could smell fresh baked food and tea brewing. Before tea, I was led to my own room, with a bathroom, and catered for my every need.

Dave and Carol invited me for a bedtime snack after I had settled. They were so interested in who I was and asked me about the run. They then spoke about their lives, including the fact that they were separated from their now adult children, who lived in Ontario. Their kids were in Ontario for work and were raising Dave and Carol's grandchildren, who had become the apple of their eyes. As we spoke, I felt so accepted and cared for, like a son returning from a semester at school. I was spoiled with food and attention. The night was a great introduction to Newfoundlanders.

The next morning, the team reassembled at the church building, spry and ready for the long drive to St. John's. My experience at Dave and Carol's had been very similar to the rest of the team's evenings with their hosts. The hospitality we had been given at Corner Brook had set the bar high, which maintained the legitimacy of the East Coast hospitality reputation. As we drove to St. John's, we imagined what our return visit to Corner Brook would be like.

After seven hours of driving on the Trans-Canada highway, we parked in downtown St. John's on Duckworth Street, right outside the famous Fred's Record store. While a few of the team members entered the store, Brittany, Tim and I had some work to do as we were facing our first problem. Our host had cancelled, which was a little bit worrisome. We were staying in St. John's for three nights and, although we had a budget for accommodations and food, I did not want to spend a large amount of it in the first week of the trip. We began calling a number of hotels and motels. We talked to three places with no luck. I was about to dial a fourth when Brittany had an idea: "Why don't I call our new contact Wanda Fost?" she suggested.

Wanda's name was given to us by World Vision. They wanted the team to have her as a contact because she had travelled across Canada eight times in the last decade, and in that time she had made hundreds of friends, some of which were in major provincial centres like St. John's. We knew it was a long shot, but Brittany decided to call Wanda anyway.

"Hi Wanda, it is Brittany Dickson from the One Nation Run."

"How are you, Brittany? I did not think you would be calling me so soon after our conversation yesterday."

"Yes, I was not expecting it either. I was wondering, Wanda, if you had any contacts in St. John's, Newfoundland? Our billets in St. John's had to cancel last minute, and right now we are parked downtown without a host for the next three nights."

Before Brittany could continue, Wanda enthusiastically responded: "Brittany, I live in St. John's! Where are you right now?"

Brittany answered: "We are downtown on Duckworth."

"Okay, well, I have to go out in fifteen minutes. So get in your cars and I'll direct you to my house."

I was a bit shocked by the turn of events, but curious to meet Wanda as few people would offer themselves to perfect strangers like she was doing for us. Within ten minutes, we pulled into Wanda's driveway. She was waiting for us at the door.

"Welcome everyone. I need to be at a meeting in five minutes, but please bring your stuff in and make yourself at home. Whatever is in the fridge and cupboards is yours to enjoy. I will return in a couple hours and then we can have a meal and get to know each other better," she said.

Wanda hugged every one of us and then vanished like a super hero. We stood dumbfounded, stunned by her trust and generosity. It took me back to my childhood and the feeling of surprise on Christmas morning. It was the ultimate gift a person could give to us in the situation we were in and, like the rest of my teammates, I responded with gratitude.

On Wanda's return home, she made us dinner, and enlightened us with laughter and words of encouragement. She gave us her home for the three days that we were in St. John's, and by the end of each day, we had been well fed, our sleepovers had been pleasant and our souls were joyful. It is hard to explain, but somehow Wanda's home had been transformed into a place for perfect strangers. What we learned in St. John's that first day was a lesson we learned throughout the trip. The lesson was also a phrase our team used a lot, especially when my father joined the team, "expect the unexpected." It was a phrase we had to embrace if we were going to fully enjoy the adventure.

* * *

It was foggy, the wind was howling and the temperature was barely above freezing at the top of Signal Hill. It was 7:45 a.m. and our team were huddled in prayer. It was May 1, the beginning of the One Nation Run. There was no media, no local runners and no crowd to cheer us on. To some degree I was disappointed, but I was more focused on my first run.

It felt a little surreal that I was actually standing at the starting line with Brittany and Zaya. I had dreamed, talked, planned, promoted and trained for this day for almost two years. Now, there I was with my two project partners, four friends and new surrogate mother about to make the One Nation Run a reality.

Like almost every run day, I began the relay on day one. This was the first of 130 and the thought of the next 8,700 kilometres to the finish line in Vancouver was daunting. I looked at Zaya, hoping he would tell me I was dreaming. He did not say much, but his vote of confidence and signature three high fives in a row confirmed that what was happening was indeed real. I shook my head and limbs to remove the daze I was in, gave the rest of the team high fives and made the descent down Signal Hill with Zaya at my side.

At the bottom of the hill stood Terry Fox's memorial marker, signifying where Terry began his trek. It was a simple brown stone marker standing roughly three feet high, which read: "Terry Fox Marathon of Hope Mile 0." We realized Terry was much wiser than us to start at the bottom of the hill as the steep decline was not the ideal way to warm up your joints for a long run. The temperature at the bottom of the hill was warmer, so I decided to take off a couple layers of clothing. Zaya stopped running to let me do the first leg solo as planned. I jogged off with Newfoundland and Canada stretching out before me. Although there was only one local supporter present at the start of the run, Wanda represented the province and her presence was invaluable.

After I finished eleven kilometres, Tim began his fifteen kilometres under a grey sky. Zaya would run a swift ten kilometres, followed by Julie who would run ten kilometres, six by Adam, five by Daphne and three by Brittany. The relay would conclude on day one in similar fashion to almost every day, with me running my second leg, which was ten kilometres. This order would give us a complete 70-kilometre relay throughout all of Newfoundland.

Our 70-kilometre relay on day one took us to Holyrood. The winds were deafening coming off the shores of the harbour, but the view was magnificent. I had a shift in thought as I gazed out on to the ocean inlet: *This day marks the first of the One Nation Run, but also my rediscovery of my country.* Still, within my heart was a frustration that Canada had failed its children who lived in poverty. I felt like I needed the run to help me rediscover my love for Canada. As always, I was optimistic, and Newfoundland was already proving why my optimism was well-founded.

* * *

We completed our first province once we returned to the shores of Port-Au-Basques. By having the McCoys with us and having never been to Newfoundland, the time passed by quickly. Everything was so new; I was captivated as my eyes searched the surrounding area. It was as if the province was in neon lighting.

Our running was efficient and we had great camaraderie; however, the best part of the province was Newfoundlanders. In every town we stayed in – from St. John's to Corner Brook – we left thinking we were honoured guests. It was reminiscent to my trip in Rwanda in 2005 when my presence there made them feel worthy that someone would travel from such a great distance to visit their country. The feeling of respect was mutual. Newfoundlanders wanted to communicate that same message to us, especially because we were fellow Canadians.

In Port Au Basques, we boarded a ferry again, this time heading to Sydney, Nova Scotia, where we would begin our Maritime running. On the ferry, I had mixed emotions. I felt a sense of accomplishment after completing a province, but I also felt sad because I would miss Newfoundland. It would be hard for Nova Scotia to top Newfoundland's hospitality.

* * *

Nova Scotians are perceived as a down to earth, peaceful people. They enjoy music and fresh seafood. They live in picturesque historical homes, surrounded by inlets and forests. Unlike Newfoundland, Nova Scotia is perfect for agriculture with the fertile land. The many farms and green fields of Nova Scotia seem only to be matched in Canada by the Lower Mainland of British Columbia.

In each home we went to in Nova Scotia, we were served like royalty. Nova Scotians took pride in welcoming us into their towns and cities, and inviting us into their homes. Halifax is one of the few cities in Canada where drivers stop for pedestrians like it is part of their DNA. They will see tourists with maps and ask if they need help instead of waiting to be asked.

On our first night in Nova Scotia, our team shrunk in size from seven to four. The McCoys had to return to Toronto. Before Daphne, Julie and Tim departed, we squeezed out as many kilometres as we could from them. Instead of running our usual 70-kilometre relay, on day six, our team ran 122 kilometres. We coined day six the 'Big Day'. It allowed us to bank kilometres as I knew we would not be able to do 70 kilometres every day that early in the One Nation Run. After May 7, Zaya and I increased our combined distance to 45 kilometres – occasionally running 55 kilometres – a big jump from the 31 kilometres in total we did in Newfoundland.

More running meant that more food was required. Our Nova Scotian hosts were up to the challenge. When they heard that Zaya and I were burning around 2,000 calories a day, they would heap on portions of food at dinner, make bedtime snacks and packed extra granola bars and bananas in our lunches. It was like we were with our mothers. For the first time in his adult life, Zaya was gaining weight, which was needed for his wiry build.

When I was running on the windy coastal roads of Nova Scotia, I took time to be thankful for our hosts. We were meeting people for the first time every other night and yet were welcomed into their homes as if we were family. At the end of each day, all our needs – and more – had been met. Our time on Nova Scotia had been eventful.

One day when we were running northeast of Truro toward the New Brunswick border, we crossed paths with a middle-aged man who looked worse for wear as he walked on the shoulder of the road. Peter, a friend from Ottawa, had joined us in Halifax after Adam had returned home to Toronto, and we decided that it might be a good idea to meet the man before Brittany saw him, as his current condition would be likely to startle her. We pulled the vehicle over to the side of the road and got out to say hello.

"Hi there, sir," I said politely.

"What are y'all up to?" he asked with an innocent curiosity.

We told him what we were doing and he seemed to be quite surprised. "Well, you sure don't meet people running across the country every day."

We then introduced ourselves, and he did the same, "Good to meet you, guys. My name is Stephen."

"Stephen, I must tell you this area is simply beautiful," I said. "This road is out of a story book with its twists and turns, forest and coastal settings. It has to be one of the most beautiful roads in the country."

"You are right. It is a beautiful road in a beautiful place. Matter of fact, right now, since you don't know, I'll tell you: you're in God's country."

The three of us nodded our heads in agreement. The beauty of the land and the hospitality in Nova Scotia was divine. That day, Stephen showed that Maritime hospitality happens in and outside of the home.

As we entered New Brunswick, we began to wonder if the hospitality only got better the longer we stayed on the East Coast. We tried not to expect that New Brunswick would top what we had just experienced. In fact, we lowered our expectations so that there was no disappointment. After all, we were staying with complete strangers and all of them were graciously letting us stay in their homes, and in many cases, were feeding us meals, too.

In every town and home from Sackville to Edmundston, we were welcomed like family. We relished the experience and were eager to express our gratitude. We were overwhelmed by our hosts' generosity.

In Fredericton, we discovered a friendly competition between Nova Scotia and New Brunswick. We found this out after we told a lady about our encounter with Stephen and him calling Nova Scotia 'God's Country'. After hearing our story, the woman smiled and said, "Well, you might have been in 'God's Country,' but you're in the 'Promised Land' now!"

The hospitality competition did not bother me any. I was happy to witness it and reap the benefits too. Upon hearing our stories about our time in Newfoundland and Nova Scotia, our hosts in New Brunswick decided to one up their rival provinces. There are few gifts that are better than delicious food for someone that just ran twenty plus kilometres.

We stayed in Fredericton for two nights, and on the second night, Eric, a friend of ours from Oakville, Ontario, joined the relay. Eric ran with us from Fredericton to Montreal. While he was with the team, we reached our 70-kilometre goal every day.

In Fredericton, our team was hosted by Marc-Etienne and Manon Hostetller, who were parents to three young children. They were an energetic family and were used to hosting travellers, especially students from South America who were on exchange. When we were with the Hostetllers, a young lady was staying with them for the school year from Venezuela.

Our team had a lot in common with Marc and Manon. We became fast friends mainly because of what was most important to us: our faith. After dinner on the first evening, Manon asked why we had decided to do what we did. I first gave the standard answer: "Because I met some of the most vulnerable children in our country, and I believed their story needed to be told."

She, however, thought there was something more and asked, "But what is driving you, what is your heart's motivation?" An intense question for some, yet for me, it was the kind of question that I would be asking. I enjoy small talk; however, I love to talk about the thing that matters most to people.

I answered Manon simply by saying, "It is my faith in Jesus that drives me to tell the children's story." I continued, "I want His love to be experienced by them, and sometimes the most powerful way to show His love is when people love others despite social, economic, religious or geographical differences."

When Manon heard this, she was more engaged, and so grew our bond with the Hostettlers. The cause was now more important to them because as Christians our mandate was to show the love of God. We spoke into the night about our faith, and before we knew it, the clock had struck midnight and we all needed to get to bed.

The next evening, Marc had an announcement he wanted to make. "This summer, I have two weeks free to do anything." We all waited thinking he was going to tell his family that they were going on a once in a lifetime vacation. Instead he said, "With that two weeks I would like to travel with the One Nation Run to wherever they need a fourth teammate the most. So where do you need another team member?" He asked us.

Brittany and Zaya had huge smiles on their faces while they waited for me to answer. Still shocked, I took a deep breath, "Wow, umm . . . how about from Regina to Edmonton at the end of August?"

There was a moment of pondering from Marc and then, "You got it! I will be there with you guys." It was an outrageous offer and one we would not refuse. It was the greatest symbol of partnership anyone gave to us in the Atlantic region and a massive sacrifice of finances and time away from his family.

The stories of families transforming their lives and homes into a refuge for us did not stop in Fredericton. In each town, families showered us with kindness and affection. There was never a day we felt alone on the East Coast. There was never a day we did not feel accepted. Many times, host families did not even ask what our needs were, but gave to us abundantly knowing what we needed.

What we experienced on the East Coast is what our hope for the One Nation Run was all about. The capacity and generosity of Canadians was incredible. And that same capacity exists, waiting to be tapped into for the children in this country who need it the most. If all Canadian kids could feel every day how we felt during our time on the East Coast, the hospitality of the East Coast would not just be legendary for visitors, it would be transformational for the entire country.

CHAPTER SIX: The Realities of the Road

BEFORE 2011, EIGHT CANADIANS HAD SUC-cessfully run across Canada. Of the two most famous journeys, one ended in Thunder Bay and the other was completed in a wheelchair. There have been books written about Terry Fox and Rick Hansen's cross-Canada treks, but there has yet to be a manual published on how to run across Canada. Crossing the vast land of the north is an adventure full of the unexpected. Our team, however, was not just running across Canada, we were also affiliated with a charity and trying to create social change like the famous runs before us. Doing the run was going to be difficult; we knew that. We needed resources and could not change society by ourselves. I knew in leading the One Nation Run that we could not be naive about the challenges of the trip. I knew we were going to make mistakes. The first mistake we made: being too giddy and idealistic.

I am sure if we read Terry Fox's biography by Douglas Coupland or Rick Hansen's book it would have been sobering. Both would have given us insights on team work, possible road and running trials and would even have described the emotions one carries when they are travelling for a cause. But reading either book would have added wood to our already blazing fire of patriotism and child-like belief in our cause. Maybe a manual would have helped ground us. However, the best cure for our hyper-optimism was the road itself. The road would bring adventure and education, but it would also be hard, and at times, unforgiving. On the road, the team received many reality checks. It acted like an alarm bell, waking me up from the daydreaming I was doing in the first month of the One Nation Run.

REALITY CHECK #1: Check your ego at the door

WHEN REALITY STRIKES, IT IS LIKE YOUR parents turning on the light in your room at six in the morning. You know you have to wake up, but the light burns your eyes. In life, we get so caught up in our expectations that we do not see the reality around us. It was in Nova Scotia that the reality of the One Nation Run hit me square in the ego.

Our journey from St. John's to Parrsboro, Nova Scotia had been adventurous and heartwarming. We experienced wonderful surprises and met dozens of incredible people. However, in regards to our mission of raising funds, building awareness through the media and compelling hundreds of people to run with us in each province, we were not on track to reach our goals. At times, I felt like we were failing. Then, on one of the most beautiful days in May when we could not have felt better physically, reality hit me.

"So, I just got off the phone with World Vision, guys," I announced to Brittany and Zaya in the van while Peter was finishing his run.

"Great what did they say?" Zaya responded with expectation.

"They told us they will not be helping us with media for the entire province of Quebec."

"Really?" Brittany blurted with surprise.

"Yup," I said with a dejected tone.

World Vision pulled the plug on promotion in Quebec because the One Nation Run name was too divisive given the sovereign movement history in that province. World Vision did not want to create any political drama and decided to keep low on the radar in order to not be a media target.

We were disappointed. I believed so passionately in the run's potential. We all thought that with hard work, good attitudes and a nationally recognized organization on our side, our mission could get into millions of Canadian homes.

How could World Vision think that by not promoting the run in the second most populated province would be a good thing? Did they not see how important our cause was? But the more I questioned their decision, the more frustrated I became.

I had to admit that I was expecting too much from Canada and World Vision. To some degree, I was blinded by pride and my infatuation to succeed, yet in spite of that, I had to take a step back and review our target and regain focus.

At night, while the team was refuelling and resting, I sought out solitude to reflect and refocus. It was a much-needed discipline, but it was not easy to maintain. We were in different homes virtually every other night, and my love for people and stories drew me to the kitchen or family room more than my own space. However, on this evening, I was able to withdraw. I needed to remember why I was on the road and who I was on the road with. There would be challenges in every province, and if I could not learn to adapt to them on the East Coast, I might not reach the West Coast – at least not with my teammates.

The reality was always – even if I was unaware of it – that we were not front page news in any major Canadian city. The One Nation Run was not even World Vision's first priority that summer. That night felt like a cold shower. Were there things legitimately worth being frustrated about? Sure. But in a beautiful country home in Sackville, that was not what I needed to be thinking about in order to lead the One Nation Run.

REALITY CHECK #2: The Adaptability of the Human Body

PRIOR TO THE RUN, I HAD THE PRIVILEGE of speaking with extreme distance runner Ray Zahab, who also lives in the Ottawa area. Ray runs in extreme climates running 50 to 70 kilometres a day for four to eight weeks at a time. Ray has run in Antarctica, the Saharan desert, the Amazon and the Andes Mountains. He runs in severe climates to educate young students about the environment and the strength of the human body and spirit. He has a team to video his running, and on breaks, he will use Skype or video blogs to discuss environmental concerns. For more on Ray, visit his website, www.rayzahab.com and his organizations website, www.impossible2possible.com.

One of the things Ray told me on the phone was that my body would quickly adapt to the long distances and strengthen and recover quicker than ever before. He said to me, "Bryce, I know you are planning to run 21 kilometres a day. I guarantee you will be running around 30 kilometres a day by the halfway point. It is not that you will want or plan to, you just will because your body will be able to."

In my training, I never felt like my body got to a level that would allow me to increase my distance. I pushed myself for six months in training. I knew I was getting stronger, but it took a lot of effort and discipline. What Ray said to me sounded great, and I hoped he was right, but I had my doubts. Wisdom, however, comes with experience, and when it came to long distance running, Ray was wise. My body did indeed respond.

In the first week, I ran 21 kilometres a day. I then ran 25 kilometres a day, beginning in Nova Scotia. I did this out of necessity as I could not recruit many runners in the province. In New Brunswick, I ran 27 kilometres a day until the day before Montreal, when I ran two days in a row of fifteen kilometres because I strained my right calf – I made the mistake of not warming up on a cool morning in Quebec City. From London to Sarnia, I ran 30 kilometres mostly because I could, and then I consistently ran 30 kilometres a day beginning in Huntsville a week and a half before the halfway point, which was Sault Ste. Marie.

Zaya's body responded much like mine. IIis perfect, long distance running build helped and so too did his competitive spirit. Zaya began at ten kilometers a day and by Huntsville his distance had reached 25 kilometers a day.

REALITY CHECK #3: "You only get to do this once."

I REMEMBER ONE NIGHT IN OTTAWA — during the months I was training for the run — Catherine and I had a blunt conversation. She was preparing me for what would be seven months on the road, most of that time being without her.

"Bryce, I am so proud of you and believe in you and what you are doing," she said.

"Thanks, Catherine, you saying that means a lot to me and gives me the freedom to put all of myself into the run, the team and the mission."

Before I could say more, Catherine continued: "I do want you to know something though."

"Sure, what's that?"

"You only get to do this once," she said with authority.

"What do you mean?"

"This whole crossing the country thing. It is wonderful what you are doing but unless I get to go with you and someone is willing to pay both of us a salary, there is no way you are doing this kind of project again."'

I paused, smiled and said, "Fair enough, my love. I will only do this once."

It was a fact that very few people crossed Canada by plane or car, let alone on foot, and such feats had only ever been accomplished on few occasions. Before 2011, only eight people had successfully ran across Canada, yet in 2011, there were seven cross Canada runs including the One Nation Run. There were days when we wanted to give up, complaining about something we did or did not do; nevertheless, when we stopped and thought about the big picture, we were reminded about our passion to succeed.

On the road, we realized how easy it could have been for us to cancel or stop the relay. I knew of three cross-Canada runs that did not finish in 2010 and 2011 because the runner had suffered a major injury. Aside from the risk of injuries, all it would take would be for one driver to make a mistake on these busy highways and that would be it.

Getting only one chance to run from coast to coast was something I did not take for granted, not even on the worst of days. I was thankful for the chance and tried to make the most of it with Brittany and Zaya.

REALITY CHECK #4: "Home is where your feet are."

QUEBEC WAS A BEAUTIFUL PLACE TO RUN. It is appropriately named "La Belle Provence." The One Nation Run route followed the St. Lawrence River from Rivière-du-Loup to Montreal. The sights were heavenly. Without any promotion, we got to relax and soak up the sights and sounds. Peter took a tour of a winery, I admired the Francophone accent, Brittany would sun tan, Zaya reflected and wrote in his journal, and Eric ran on nearby trails right on the shores of the St. Lawrence. The first week in Quebec was serene.

In contrast to the Atlantic region, our stays with our hosts were longer. We had fewer connections in Quebec, partly due to the language barrier and because I could not make as many church connections. From a project goal perspective, the Quebec stretch was a lowlight. We raised literally all our Quebec funds in Montreal and had a single interview and only one speaking engagement, both of which took place in Montreal. There were, however, many more elements to our reality on the road in Quebec.

To be in Quebec was to be in the most romantic province of Canada; to be amongst the most fashionable people and to be able to savour the richest of foods and drink, and to be surrounded by the most passionate political citizens in the country. Despite stereotypes portrayed in the media, every person we met from Quebec was proud to be Canadian. To be in Quebec meant I could easily feel at home.

The people we stayed with were wonderfully different from one another and different from most people we met on the East Coast. In Rivière-du-Loup, we stayed with a young Francophone couple that struggled to speak English. In Quebec City, we stayed with Zaya's aunt and uncle who were once immigrants from the Democratic Republic of Congo, now happy Canadian citizens. In Trois-Rivières, we stayed with an Acadian couple who were bilingual and settled in a farming community on the south side of the St. Lawrence in the early 1980s. Our hosts all treated us so well and gave us a beautiful portal into Quebec living. At the end of our stay, we tasted the best, saw the best and met the best of Quebec.

In Montreal, we had worked it out with the local police that we would receive a police escort through the city. I was extremely enthusiastic about it because it showed tremendous generosity by the police, especially since we were not from Montreal or even Quebec. However, the day before we were scheduled to run through Montreal, the officer I was planning the relay with called and cancelled the escort. He apologized profusely, but told me that he had made an error in judgement and remembered a large bicycle race was being held in the city the same day and the officers he had assigned to lead the escort were on duty for the race. On top of the escort not being available, the officer told me the route for the bicycle race. It happened to have similar roads as our relay, which meant the One Nation Run would have to be re-routed. It was a huge setback, but there was nothing I could do except plan something different.

I was on the computer and the phone until eleven at night, orchestrating the changes with friends from Montreal. The detour I created had our relay going through the north end of the city and then curling down the west end of the west island before arriving in Dorval, where the relay would end. The planning exhausted me, and when my head finally hit the pillow, I was out as fast as the lights when the switch was flicked.

By the time I woke up the following morning, I had received many emails and text messages asking to clarify the changes by those participating in the relay from Montreal. At ten o'clock that morning, everyone was ready to begin and at the end of the relay, my friends Tammy and Paul, were waiting for us with many of their friends who were also runners and excited about what we were doing. In total, there were about 60 people of whom 35 participated in the relay. Tammy, Paul and their church had prepared a large meal for everyone. When the relay and meal were finished, Paul interviewed Zaya and I so that we could share why we were running and answer any questions about our journey to that point.

Like the tables in Newfoundland, I found satisfaction that day in a Dorval park on the banks of the St. Lawrence. Sitting with 60 people under a clear evening sky, I experienced acceptance and a sense of belonging. I felt at home with Tammy, Paul and Lakeshore Evangelical Church that night. In Montreal, Quebec, and across the country, a reality of the road was that home was never far away, it was where our feet were.

REALITY OF THE ROAD
#5: Poverty is ubiquitous

THE REASON WHY I WAS ON THE ROAD WAS because I wanted to share the story of Amy with as many people as possible. In the eastern half of the country, because school was still in session, I had opportunities to tell Amy's story in a dozen schools. Every time I shared her story with children and youth, they were surprised. Canadian children were genuinely upset that Amy and her friends lived life the way they did. In almost every classroom, students wanted to know how they could help their peers because they believed poverty was 'un-Canadian'.

But there were more stories than just Amy's, and as the One Nation Run travelled through the eastern half of the country, I saw other children living in unacceptable circumstances. Their financial needs were not as grave as those in communities like Amy's, but they still lived in 'un-Canadian' conditions – not glorious and free. Before the trip, I knew the statistics: one in ten Canadian children lived in poverty. I also knew the places that were really struggling, many of which were in New Brunswick. But when I saw the faces of the many impoverished children, the statistics had meaning, and therefore I was compelled to tell their stories.

In each province, and almost every town or city neighbourhood, we would meet children who were suffering in a way that no child should. In some cases, it was more than just bad parenting decisions; it was plain bad luck. In Port Hawkesbury, Nova Scotia dozens of jobs were being lost each month. In Saint John, there were whole neighbourhoods living in cyclical poverty. The city had warehouses and factories closed down and drugs and prostitution had increased over the last 40 years. Because of its high unemployment rate and lack of business or industrial innovation, Saint John is now one of Canada's poorest urban centres. On top of Saint John's struggles, Statistics Canada reported that New Brunswick had seven of Canada's poorest communities.

As we entered Quebec, poverty continued to rear its ugly head. It was most obvious in cities like Montreal and Trois-Rivières. In the cities of Quebec, there are whole neighbourhoods that collect welfare. Children in those neighbourhoods learn at early ages that it is okay to be dependent on the government.

In these places, children are being born into families with absent fathers and teenage mothers. In major Canadian cities like Montreal and Toronto, there are also large populations of refugee families. These families come to Canada to escape the horrors and destruction of war, religious persecution and genocide. When they enter Canada, they have only a few dollars to their name and the clothes on their back. Their decision to immigrate to Canada was not based on wanting to find better education and work, it was based on survival – something most Canadians can't comprehend. But these were just a few of the stories we heard on the road; it was the pictures of the children that stayed in our minds. Like Amy and her peers in Central Manitoba, the children we met on the road were not easily forgotten, and as such, gave us the added motivation we needed to continue on our journey.

Before school was out for summer, the team and I talked to as many schools, churches, families and journalists as we could. We asked Canadians to look in their neighbourhoods and towns for children who were struggling and seek to help them through friendship. Poverty was too common a reality on the road, and yet it was a problem not being confronted by individual Canadian families and schools in wealthy neighbourhoods.

We used our platform of cross country runners to bring the children's reality into the homes of wealthier Canadian families so they were forced to come face to face with the sadness and suffering that existed. It was not always comfortable for us as we told the stories, but we were compelled to tell them nevertheless. It was uncomfortable for families and schools to hear the stories, yet without such knowledge, then nothing would change and we, as a nation, would continue to fail our most vulnerable citizens.

GLORIOUS AND FREE: PART 2

CHAPTER SEVEN: Discovery Kids

I HAVE WATCHED MANY SHOWS ON TERRY Fox and I have always thought of him as one of Canada's greatest role models. His courage and strength are equal to any soldier or activist. Obviously Terry is best known for his 'Marathon of Hope' when he ran 42 kilometres every day until his body could not run anymore. We all can envision his unique stride and imagine how much effort and determination must have gone into climbing a hill or running into a merciless wind. However, there was another part of Terry's journey from St. John's to Thunder Bay that stands out for me and is well documented: his love for children. In many towns and cities, Terry met children who would run with him. Children received great inspiration from Terry, but Terry admitted the children were a great source of inspiration to him.

While I crossed Canada with the team I saw many monuments of Terry that captured his powerful story and enduring spirit. Many of the roads we ran on, Terry had run on before us. We were happy to be in his shadow. After our second day of running, our connection to Terry got even closer. The run ended at Arnold's Cove, Newfoundland. It was a quaint little village right on the ocean shores. Like so many of our nights in Newfoundland we were spoiled by our hosts, and on that particular night we were treated to a full turkey dinner. We then received another treat when we discovered the son-in-law of our hosts, who was present at dinner, had run with Terry Fox as a child. He ran with

Terry side by side for a few hundred metres, along with a half dozen or so classmates who were eager to shake Terry's hand. The man we met was now in his forties, yet he remembered his encounter with Terry vividly and held him with the highest regard. Although their meeting had been short, the great man had left a mark on him. He spoke often of their encounter and that he believed that he had been in the presence of greatness.

While we ran coast to coast, children impacted us every day. There were some speaking engagements at schools where we felt like celebrities and heroes, but most of the time we left with greater inspiration and encouragement because of their energy, enthusiasm and perseverance in their own situation. I can recall speaking with a grade five and a six class in Elsipogtog, New Brunswick about child poverty. This was a group of students that was living in one of Canada's poorest communities. But when asked about whom they thought of when they heard the words 'child poverty' they referred to children living in Haiti. "They have suffered so much because of the earthquake," they told us. "And don't forget the children in Japan. A Tsunami destroyed their houses." When we spoke to the children about child poverty in Canada they still never once thought about their own circumstances. The children's focus on others was exemplary and compelled me to speak of them to other people across Canada.

In Halifax we stayed with a family with two children, aged ten and thirteen years old. They both were influential in their schools and raised thousands of dollars for communities in developing countries to have clean drinking water. The two kids ran with us for eleven kilometres combined, but their hard work stayed with us until we reached Vancouver.

June 18 was an amazing day. The One Nation Run travelled 70 kilometres from the Toronto/Mississauga border to Jerseyville, a small town just west of Hamilton. The morning was warm, the afternoon was scorching. The sun was bright and we were thankful for the breeze that came off Lake Ontario and the shadows of the large maple and oak trees. The day was the team's homecoming and we soaked it up. The previous night we all slept in our own beds and our families lavished with love, making our favourite meals and giving us special gifts to show how proud they were of us. During the morning run through Mississauga, we were joined by the Peel regional police who escorted us to Oakville, which was in the next town. Also in Mississauga we were greeted by over 150 people including 50 runners. I had the privilege of running beside World Vision Canada's Vice President, Michael Messenger. Michael was gracious enough to join me for ten kilometres and then ran another ten with Zaya to incarnate World Vision's solidarity with the One Nation Run. He represents World Vision well.

At times during the homecoming I felt like a teenager again. There was so much interest and encouragement from my family and the church. It was like I was being sent off to university or cheered on during a sporting event. For that morning the world felt like a perfect place.

As the relay continued through Oakville I drove with Catherine who was with our team for the weekend. It was incredible to witness the support of my community. There was still more to do that day, but I had to savour the moment.

My second ten kilometres that day would be with a fourth grader from Burlington named Craig. I was connected to Craig by his teacher Mrs. Jansz, who also happens to be a friend of mine. Mrs. Jansz had said Craig looked up to Terry Fox and was an elite runner in his school board. Craig placed second in Halton Region in cross country and in the middle distance track events. When Mrs. Jansz told Craig about what I was doing he asked if he could meet me. Mrs. Jansz said, "Meet Bryce? Craig, I think if you would like, you could run with Bryce?" Craig thought that was a fantastic idea. Mrs. Jansz emailed me in the spring, before the run had started and had me correspond with Craig's mother to organize a time Craig could run with me. Craig's mom said Craig would be delighted and we agreed that Craig would run five kilometres with me in Burlington.

When I met Craig along Lakeshore Road I was a little worried about whether or not he could run five kilometres, especially in the heat of the day. Craig's mom was pretty confident that he would finish and just asked that we take an extra water break. Craig was a typical grade four boy and was much more excited in doing something than talking about it. Before we began our run I warmed up, and soon after, Mrs. Jansz and her husband arrived to cheer Craig on. It really gave Craig a boost to see Mrs. Jansz. For the second time that day – at least for me and my old legs – we took off. Craig must have thought we were being timed because he ran the first two and a half kilometres to the first water break quickly. While we ran the first section Craig never slowed down and where ever there was a low branch from one of the large trees he jumped to try to hit it. When we reached the first water break Craig took two sips of water and then looked to me eager to continue running. The second stretch was just as fast but now Craig was talking more about his running and inquiring as to why I decided to run across Canada. When I told him what the run was about he mentioned a couple of kids at his school who at times did not have lunch or proper winter clothing. Near the end of our run he asked me if he could run the next five kilometres with me – like I said, he was an elite runner.

I was deeply impressed by Craig and the energy he radiated, which would help me while I continued on my journey.

We had completed the ten-kilometre run in under 50 minutes. For us, that was not such a big deal, as we were focused on being as efficient and professional as possible. However, for the average person, to run such distances in this heat, then that would be a different matter entirely. Craig was in grade four and had never run more than five kilometres before, and therefore what he had accomplished was quite extraordinary. After Craig had had some water, we had our photo taken together. He was a sensational young man – a running prodigy – but more importantly, he was sensitive and empathetic. His mom could not have been prouder.

The next day we ran from Jerseyville to London, Ontario. It was another hot day so we tried to get on the road before nine in the morning to beat some of the heat. June 19 was the twelfth running day my dad had participated in. My dad had signed up to travel with the team from June 6 to July 3rd, starting in Montreal and ending in Huntsville, Ontario. He is a kid at heart, even at 65 years old. He kept the team light, helping us to live in the moment and not take ourselves too seriously. He also made sure we had many treats, stopping for chocolate milk at convenience stores and French fries at chip trucks along the way.

What was amazing about my dad's involvement on the road was that two years prior to the One Nation Run, he had had major open heart surgery to replace a valve. Two months before his surgery he was bench pressing 250 pounds and training to run a half marathon. My dad, in many ways, had always been like Superman to me. Eight days after surgery he was struggling to walk ten metres in the hospital. It was difficult to see him without his cape.

However, when he was on the road with us he ran five or six kilometres a day in some of the hottest days of the run. He never complained and even had mini competitions with himself to see if he could beat his personal best time once a week. Sunday June 19, 2011, was Father's Day. Like so many days in my life my dad was again supporting me as best he knew how, by showing up and being involved in what I was doing. I was so thankful and proud to be his son.

Also on Father's Day, another father, Tim Carver, ran with the team. Tim was going to run five kilometres as well, but he would not run by himself. Beside him for a couple of kilometres was his thirteen-year-old daughter, Amelia. Amelia had raised money at her school by selling One Nation Run T-shirts and promoted the run in her neighbourhood. The previous day we had ran through

Mississauga she had cheered the team on with her whole family, and she was delighted to discover that her dad was going to participate in the run the next day. The One Nation Run meant a lot to her, so much so, she wrote a paper on the team, about how we were her heroes.

That year before the One Nation Run, Brittany actually lived with the Carver family. Amelia and Brittany had many conversations about children living in our country who did not have clean drinking water and other basic needs. But Amelia did not just look up to us for what we were doing; she had the will and passion to support us. Her commitment to our cause brought optimism and hope that other children and youth would embrace the message. When we spoke at a school we knew that there would be 'Amelias' in the room that would not just say "Wow", but would ask, "How can I help?" Hearing her talk about her fundraising campaign and seeing her run beside her dad was life giving.

We had the blues on Tuesday morning, June 21. We already missed not being with our friends and family. We would get another dose of homecoming on July 1 when we would cross Toronto on the north side before going north to Barrie, but after the parade-type atmosphere, we felt like we had a bit of a "Homecoming Hangover." The week of the 21st would have its great moments including the celebration of Zaya's 26th birthday. We actually celebrated Zaya's birthday three times that week. However, even with the celebrations it was nothing like our previous week. Instead of averaging twenty runners a day we would only average two extra runners per day. It was a sobering reality that our highest support level was behind us. Still, the week from London to Sarnia was a more accurate reflection of the run and we received some support and media attention in other areas of the country, but nowhere near what we got within a two-hour radius of Toronto.

On July 6 we ran under overcast skies on the shoulder of Highway 11. It was a long and lonely road. It was the beginning of weeks of similar days. After Southwestern Ontario we had reunited with some more friends, supporters and media. We played in the water after runs at friends' cottages, and enjoyed BBQs all the way to Muskoka. But things changed and very quickly. A day's run north of Huntsville, support and media was bleak; in fact, I remember a feeling of heaviness when we left Huntsville toward North Bay as if we were carrying the full weight of the mission. It felt like we were entering into a wilderness, or at least a loneliness we had yet to experience. When we spoke about what might be the most difficult stretch of the trip, both Zaya and I felt strongly that it would be Northern Ontario. We called Huntsville "The Point of No Return." Huntsville was our last chance to turn around and confess we could not handle the project, the grind of living out of suitcases and sleeping in different beds every night. Being close to our home town kept us grounded; however, in Central and Northern Ontario, we were in unfamiliar territory.

In Northern Ontario we saw more wildlife than people and often there were times we had no reception with our internet stick or cell phones. For the first time on our journey I was having doubts. Would I be able to lead effectively? Would our bodies and minds endure the wear and tear of being on the road? Would our mission and message lose momentum? The first night north of Huntsville we slept in a hotel room. In fact, we slept in more hotels and motel rooms in Northern Ontario than anywhere else in the country. I became increasingly concerned about our budget. Would we have enough money to get to Vancouver?

During our time from North Bay to Thunder Bay, two friends joined us for a week each: Greg from Toronto and Paul from Montreal. They both gave our team a much needed familiar face and a lift of optimism. They also brought with them encouragement from back home. Greg even had baked goods from his mom. They told us that we were not alone on our journey. People were praying for us and cheering us on. I was comforted by their presence and words.

The last fifteen kilometres on July 16 was when I experienced a breakthrough. The team had spent some quality time in Sault Ste. Marie, with a lovely woman called Ruth, and now we were back into the forest of Northern Ontario. While I was finishing the relay of the day I ran through a small inlet called Montreal River Harbour. The inlet was at the bottom of a steep two and a half kilometre hill, a hill that had completely exhausted Terry Fox when he had ran up it. The owner of the camp ground we stayed at that evening told us that he had been a reporter when Terry Fox was running. Terry told the man that it was the first hill that he had been intimidated by. Just by looking at it I could tell I needed to be determined to summit it. It was at that moment I decided to dig inside my mind and soul and unearth the doubt that was planted there. To do so I chose to remember the children I was running for. As I climbed the hill I felt the strain of my legs and lungs. In my mind, however, I was thinking about what the kids might be doing if they were in my shoes. I began to think like a kid looking around at the great outdoors. At one point I even stopped to look back onto Lake Superior. It was like an ocean as the lake went as far as the horizon. I marvelled at its different shades of blue and then turned to admire the rock faces of cliffs around me. My imagination grew when I thought about coming face to face with the "Sleeping Giant" of Thunder Bay and the giant goose of Wawa. I thought about Craig and Amelia being right where I was and how they would respond to the beauty of my surroundings. In being childlike I discovered this part of my country in a new and innocent way and it gave me hope to continue and push through to the top of the hill and through the loneliness and doubt.

In total, we had spent 57 days in Ontario, running on 49 of them and covering over 3,400 kilometres. We spent more days discovering Ontario than all four previous provinces combined.

From North Bay until we arrived in Winnipeg there were only two cities, Thunder Bay and Sudbury. There were more people in my home city than all the people combined in Northern Ontario. There was so much to discover, much of it was different from Mississauga and unique to Northern Ontario.

Our last stop in Ontario was Kenora. It is home to many NHL hockey players' cottages and a generous family, the Birds. Our team was linked with the Birds through a host in Sault Ste. Marie. We were struggling to find any connections in Kenora and when we did we did not hesitate to ask if we could stay with them. The Birds obliged.

Catherine, who had joined us again in Thunder Bay, arrived with the whole team at the Bird family house hungry and thirsty after we had experienced another long week on the road. We were so happy to be housed by a family as we had spent the last two nights in hotel rooms in Ignace and Dryden. Because we were such city people and we had spent so much time in remote places, we craved company and home-cooked meals, and were excited to be spending time with children.

The Bird family parents were Neil and Heather. They were an educated couple with "their feet on the ground." They really made us feel like we were at home. Heather and Neil had four boys: Eli aged two, Jo-Jo aged five, Ari aged eight and Kenan aged eleven. They were unique boys who all carried stereotypical traits of their birth order. Kenan was responsible, Ari was innovative, Jo-Jo was compassionate and Eli was an admirer of his older brothers. The dynamics between the four brothers was all the entertainment one needed. Each day Heather would make feasts and delegated responsibilities. Kenan barbequed on the first night, Jo-Jo would retrieve eggs for breakfast from the chicken pen out back and Ari made sure the table was set and that everyone knew when it was meal time. Heather ran a tight ship. Each day we spent with the Birds we learned more about them and they learned more about us. Jo-Jo who was as curious as George and asked many questions, while Ari took copious notes and recorded them verbatim in his mind, at times recalling our exact words.

From the beginning of the run we invited people to participate in what we were doing. We believed the more people who were involved the greater the mission and message would be. People could practically help us in four ways: house us, share our story, run with us, and donate to World Vision's Canadian programming. The Birds had been amazing at the first two until one of the family members decided he wanted his family to complete the "One Nation Run cycle."

On the Tuesday afternoon of our visit Ari made an announcement to the team. Ari told us that he wanted to run to the train tracks and back in solidarity of the One Nation Run and donate a toonie just as our website, which he already read, said participants were asked to do. My eyebrows raised, but with Heather's permission I certainly would not stand in Ari's way. So, before dinner Ari ran to the railway crossing and back for a total of two kilometres. I travelled in the vehicle with Catherine who was filming Ari's run.

When Ari was finished Jo-Jo made an announcement at the dinner table: "After dinner, I will run to the train tracks and back and donate a toonie to your cause." We were all pretty impressed. After dinner we jumped back in the car except Zaya who joined Jo-Jo for the run.

I was touched by the sign of solidarity Ari and Jo-Jo made. The run was influencing children to exercise and be unselfish with money. On the Wednesday after our run, the two brothers ran another two kilometres each and even donated another two dollars, this time in quarters. We were stunned by their dedication to our team and cause.

On Thursday morning we all said our goodbyes. We all had long faces and were sad to be parting company. We knew how much the Birds had sacrificed to have hosted the four of us at their home and knew how much they were a part of our team.

However, it would not be the last time we would see the Birds. Weeks after we left Kenora, Heather sent me a note asking if we could visit the boys' school and share the story of our journey. Naturally we appreciated the invitation and visited each of Jo-Jo, Ari and Kenan classes on our way back. The invitation, however, was not nearly the most powerful compliment or sign of partnership our team received from the Bird family. Later in Heather's email, she explained how Ari and Jo-Jo had been captivated by what we were doing. Ari and Jo-Jo had run two kilometres every day that the One Nation Run ran after we left Kenora and continued to donate as much as they could. As I read Heather's note I welled up. I leaned back in my chair and thought of the boys' efforts and how truly compassionate and devoted they were to us. They were not just kids we met that we had a few laughs with or shared a good meal with; they were our teammates on the road, sharing in our sacrifice and vision for our country.

On Thursday, October 6, Zaya and I pulled into the boys' school. Heather was with us when we met the principal, and when we arrived at each of the classrooms, Kenan, Ari and Jo-Jo were proud to show us off. We were proud too. We explained what we were doing and why, and Ari told his class anything we forgot to say, including giving a plug for our website: "There is a blog Bryce wrote about Kenora called 'Kenora Keep Shining.' It really is worth reading. While you are on the website you can also donate to their charity." When we were in Jo-Jo's class he made sure to tell Zaya how much it meant to him that we had come. As Zaya sat down with him on the kindergarten class carpet, Jo-Jo thanked him, in which Zaya told him that it was his pleasure to be with him again. What the boys did not know, is that when we travelled across the prairies and the mountains we spoke about them to families, classrooms and reporters.

In Ari, Jo-Jo, Amelia and Craig we had found the children we were looking for to carry our message of "Glorious and Free." Each of them in their own way had given us so much of themselves in such a small period of time. As much as our run might have impacted them, their support had a lasting impact on us. After meeting them and being around all of them I was not the same runner or communicator. They gave me greater confidence, not only that we would see the shores of the Pacific in Vancouver, but that the dream and the work of the One Nation Run would live on in Canadian children. What I discovered in Ontario was that the next generation was already rising up with compassion and creativity to bring light to places where lights were burning dim.

CHAPTER EIGHT: Second Wind

I GREW UP IN THE CITY OF MISSISSAUGA, on the border of Toronto, which is the biggest city in Canada. My grandparents lived in Toronto, on the west side of the downtown and within walking distance of the subway. I thoroughly enjoyed visiting them, first and foremost because of our love for each other, but outside of the relationship because I thought Toronto, the big city, was so fascinating and fun. On my grandparents' street, Lansdowne Avenue, the houses were closer together and people of different cultures lived beside each other. When I visited my grandparents the smells and sounds from many Western European countries could be experienced. As a boy who loved sports, visiting Toronto meant I would be closer to my sports heroes. My favourite sport when I was a little kid was baseball, which meant I was also a huge Toronto Blue Jays fan. I went to the last game ever played at Exhibition Stadium and was in the dome with my cousin Clark, when Joe Carter hit his famous World Series winning home run. In the hay days of the Jays the city rallied around the team and I loved being in the middle of the celebrations. To me, Toronto was like the centre of the universe with so many people and so many things happening. I was definitely lured by the lights of the big city.

In my life I have lived in four places, all of which are cities: raised in Mississauga, London for university, Toronto for my first job and Ottawa where I currently reside. None were smaller than three hundred thousand people. When I travelled the world the places I found most interesting were the cities. There is natural beauty in the rural parts of the world that is breathtaking, however, I am most attracted to cities and city life: the people, the culture, the varieties of food and the sights and sounds during festivals. I rarely feel anxious in a crowd. I don't mind the noise, unless it is construction before eight in the morning. And in the city I never get bored. So a problem started to grow inside of me in mid-July on the road, I was home sick, or maybe, more accurately, I was missing the city life.

At times my energy levels were low as we ran from Huntsville, Ontario to Winnipeg. There were just not that many people. During a couple of stretches northwest of Thunder Bay, there were no homes for over 30 kilometres. Yet when I was at my lowest or most unstable, Catherine joined the team again. She pledged to run ten kilometres a day, keeping me from going any crazier than I already was. Catherine was with the One Nation Run from Thunder Bay to Winnipeg, which really kept me focused when I ran, and distracted me from feeling like we were alone in the middle of the wilderness. There were times when I almost lost it. One day near Upsala, Ontario, my mind was so weak I thought I could not finish my 30 kilometres for the day. After a few hugs, and some sweet words from Catherine – and some great "DJing" from Zaya – I was able to push myself to run 32.5 kilometres. Catherine gave me a little wind in my sails.

While I ran in Northern Ontario I was appreciative of many things – first and foremost the people. They were extraordinarily generous. Our hosts went above and beyond what we requested and the team always had great conversations with them; it made it difficult for us to leave each home. Secondly, I appreciated Lake Superior. As the biggest of the Great Lakes, Lake Superior acts like an ocean in North Ontario. Massive ships cruise the lake and dock in towns, the waves can be quite large and the sound of their crash has a calming effect on those who hear them. Its temperature is usually below fifteen Celsius, which is not ideal for most swimmers but an excellent temperature for legs to recover after running long distances. The cold water also gives some much needed humour as people try to enter into it – watching Zaya enter was particularly funny. Lastly, I appreciated the steep hills of the region, though the relationship was "love hate." The declines were steep and tough on my joints. However, the difficulty of the Northern Ontario hills prepared us for the Rocky Mountains. Looking back, Northern Ontario was the most challenging place we ran.

The remoteness of Northern Ontario meant the One Nation Run's mission was not receiving much attention. No media, topped with the fact that schools were out for summer, meant that the One Nation Run's awareness campaign was quite limited. Periodically we had newspaper interviews and a couple of radio interviews, but for the most part the message of the run was brought down to a whisper for much of July.

On August 5, the team ran into Winnipeg and I immediately got a lift when I saw the cityscape in the distance. It was wonderful to be back in a city and one with a World Vision office in town. The office took care of our media relations and set up speaking engagements.

In Winnipeg, a World Vision employee named Danny McKay had volunteered to be our chauffeur as well as our agent to make sure we talked to the right radio and television stations. We did not get any national exposure, but we did get the opportunity to speak to First Nations' youth on Streets FM, a local First Nations' radio station. When we were on the air with Streets' DJ Big Will, we told the youth that they were our inspiration for running across the country.

Danny was more than our driver, he became a friend of ours and we spent two days with him, touring the city and going to interviews and out for lunch. While we sat down for lunch at Ivory, a fine Indian restaurant and my personal favourite in Canada, Danny asked us some personal questions. It was obvious that he believed in what we were doing, but wanted to make sure we were doing well as individuals, too. As Zaya and I ran the bulk of kilometres each day and were in the spotlight during interviews and in social media, it was easy to have inflated egos. On other occasions when there was no media attention and few donations I would ask myself, "Is what we are doing making a difference?" As the pendulum of emotions swung while we crossed Canada, especially in the drastic change from Northern Ontario to Winnipeg, it was important that we spoke as human beings, not just social activists.

Winnipeg gave more to us than just media attention and personal grounding—it refocused us. Just north of the city was where my life had changed in 2008 when I met the children of Little Saskatchewan. The memories of that trip and the two others to Central Manitoba took centre stage in my mind during our stay in Winnipeg. It was the same for Zaya and Brittany who travelled on the winter roads in Central Manitoba, Zaya in 2009 and Brittany in 2011. The stories and faces of the children replayed in our minds.

Before the run began I had strategically decided to give our team a three-day rest in Winnipeg. I knew Northern Ontario would be taxing and anticipated the need to refocus. As part of our time off I thought it would be appropriate to visit Little Saskatchewan. Zaya and Brittany had never been and I had not been back since 2010. However, our trip to Little Saskatchewan was cancelled after flood waters forced the people of the community to abandon their homes in the spring of 2011. The community could not return to their homes because of the extent of the water damage for over a year. Despite building a promising future out of a troubled past, once again Little Saskatchewan came up against difficult circumstances. Almost on a daily basis we prayed for Little Saskatchewan, and throughout the run we carried them in our hearts and wrote about their struggles in blogs, Facebook statuses and journals.

It was in Winnipeg where I had to re-examine the run's objective. It would have been easy to have stayed in Winnipeg and try to increase media attention and support for Little Saskatchewan in a time of need. What helped was that I got to see Rick and Liz Greer on the Friday night. They had returned to Winnipeg with ten people from my old church in Mississauga. On the Saturday they would pick up another team from another church to lead the last of six summer camp weeks at the sixth First Nations community. Rick and Liz were happy to see the team. We all asked how the summer was going and how we could support one another. Rick and Liz were fully behind us. Their support mattered to me, especially that night. Here was a couple who knew the people of Little Saskatchewan and they were encouraging us to press on and finish the mission and journey we had begun. It was difficult to move forward when I thought about how the children of Little Saskatchewan had been living away from their homes for over three months, but Rick and Liz helped me find peace with the knowledge that what I was doing was a worthy cause.

And so we did rest. Our team took the next three days to rest our legs and recalibrate our minds for the mission. The rest for both body and mind was important as it reminded us that we were not super heroes or saviours, we alone were not going to end child poverty in Canada. The rest forced us to acknowledge what we could do and remain positive, and turn our minds away from any negativity.

On the Saturday the whole team relaxed, which for me meant being able to go on a date with Catherine, our first date for over three months since the run began. We went for walks, picnicked for dinner, laughed and reminisced as the sun set. Yes, I know, very mushy. By the end of our five-day stay in Winnipeg, the whole team was re-energized and focused.

When people think of the prairies they think of flat land. The topography makes it possible to see all the way to the horizon in all directions. The fields of flax, wheat, canola and sunflower cut into the earth with straight lines like bathroom tiles. If a person were to bring a level and put it on the highways of the prairies more often than not the bubble would get in between the lines. So, when people think of running through the prairies, they think it will be easy because the land is so flat, and for the most part this is true; however, there is one aspect of flat farm land that people do not consider – the wind.

In Canada, the jet stream – the direction of air flow – travels west to east. At times the jet stream runs more southeast, but for the most part there is a strong head wind if you are travelling west. In addition, the prairies have very few trees let alone forests, which means there is little protection from the winds. So when the wind blows in the prairies, you are going to feel the full force.

On the Trans Canada near Moosomin, Saskatchewan, the skies were grey and the winds were running right into us at 45 kilometres an hour. As was the custom, I ran the first section. The winds were so strong, which meant that even warming up was a difficult task. The setting was intimidating. Running into the wind felt like you were on a treadmill. As I was putting one foot in front of the other, my pace was two minutes slower per kilometre. The wind was like a middle school bully, relentless, and really wore my lungs and confidence down. As a team, I questioned whether or not we would complete our relay during the daylight.

Although I was at a turtle's pace and expending an enormous amount of energy, I still managed to catch up to two cyclists. With wind gusts of over 60 kilometres an hour, I was running faster than they could cycle. At one point I asked Greg, who rejoined the team in Winnipeg, to drive the vehicle in front of me to block the wind. It was effective, but not a fuel efficient or environmentally responsible use of the vehicle. It did, however, keep me from exploding with frustration. As the day went on each team member battled the wind with increasing agitation. During my afternoon run I recall yelling at the wind, telling the wind that there was no reason to fight with me and that we could be on the same team. The agitation was escalating into delusion. At the end of our 70-kilometre relay, we were on empty. That day the wind was more tiring than the hills of Northern Ontario. After running 30 kilometres I crumbled into the back seat of the vehicle like a paper plane.

The winds returned throughout our time in Saskatchewan. They played the villain role and each day I prayed that I would not have to play the hero. When we blogged about our time in Saskatchewan, we often mentioned the wind. It was the prevailing element in the prairies. The strong winds were not the only things worth writing home about. We were also dive bombed by hawks. Between the hawks and the wind I had my doubts to whether the province really wanted us running there. Another reappearance that was made in Saskatchewan was the highly anticipated return of Fredericton, New Brunswick's Marc Hostettler. He had promised that he would join us for the trip from Regina to Edmonton. Marc was a man of his word and kept his promise.

Marc's flight was the longest of anyone who joined the team before Vancouver. It was a generous, sacrificial act because of the cost and the amount of time he would spend away from his family. In truth, it was an undertaking of generosity by the whole Hostettler family. I was thankful for Marc being with us and thanked his wife Manon when I spoke to her on the phone after I picked up Marc from the airport. There was more inspiration in Regina besides Marc joining us. In Regina we met a gentleman named Mark Newton, a friend of Danny McKay's. Mark ran in the relay the day the One Nation Run went through Regina. Mark ran eighteen kilometres with a friend named Bill. Mark had an amazing running story that actually involved Danny.

In his teenage years Mark was a trained boxer. He trained and competed and was able to win many fights. As time went on Mark's body got weaker and he had to hang up his boxing gloves. His knees were worn down from all the training. Even when he walked it caused him pain, so to move around swiftly in the ring was near impossible. More than boxing Mark missed the running component of his training. He enjoyed the endurance from long distance running, and the peace he discovered while out on the open road.

In the spring of 2010, Danny McKay visited Mark with a mutual friend. The three friends got talking about life and then Mark's knee injury came up in the conversation. Mark told his two friends how much he missed running. Danny then responded: "How would you like to be healed from your injury?"

Caught off guard Mark replied, "Come on, man, are you kidding?"

"No I am serious," Danny said with a straight face.

"How are my knees going to be healed?"

"Well, if you are willing we can all ask God to heal your knees."

"Really?"

"Yup," Danny said confidently.

After some awkward silence Mark said that he would like for his two friends to pray for his knees to be healed. They prayed for five to ten minutes. After they prayed Danny asked: "How do they feel? Do you feel anything different?"

Mark answered, "They feel a little less tight I guess and the dull pain seems to have gone away. Do you think . . .?"

"I have faith that God heard us," Danny interjected.

A month or so later Mark decided to go out for a run. He went at a slow pace. Being cautious he put on an old knee brace that he used to wear when training for boxing. The run felt good. A few days later he went for another one. After a few runs he called Danny to inform him of the good news.

"You'll never guess what I have been doing this week," Mark said.

"What's that?" Danny inquired.

"I have been doing some light running."

When we met Mark on the run he could not have been happier. In a year he had gone from not running, to running up to five kilometres with a brace, to running full marathons without a brace. He was a running miracle. While we were in Winnipeg, Danny had informed us that Mark would act like he had two new legs; he said that Mark would be bouncing, shouting with excitement and generally brimming with gratitude. To be honest Mark acted like he was given a new life. He was enthusiastic about every step. He told us about how God had healed him and how much his life had changed because of it. He was so thankful for his health, every breath and his whole life. He said it was hard to contain his joy. Mark's energy and positive outlook were contagious. His story and presence served as great motivation for the team.

Mark was a reminder that running was a luxury and that thousands of Canadians were unable to run at all. I was fortunate to be able to run with strength, freedom and enjoyment. Mark's story cleared any ounce of complaint that might have been in me and brought out more gratitude to the Creator for each step and each breath I was able to take.

In a greater way, Mark was a catalyst in understanding how lucky I was to have the opportunity I had. To run across the country was not just the journey of a lifetime, it was an amazing opportunity and I believe that there are many Canadians who have that ability to perform such a feat. There are also Canadians who have causes that they believe in and would like to travel the country telling fellow citizens about the issue that drives their life. There are many Canadians who have dreams but do not have the resources or the support system of a community or family to be able to fulfil their ambitions. There are also people who just want to see Canada from coast to coast in one shot but because of responsibilities they are unable to do so. I was presented with an amazing opportunity. The timing was good and I had the support of a great team, and therefore I could accomplish the goal of crossing Canada on foot. I obviously had the will to do it, but many people have the will and not necessarily the opportunity. I did not want to take it for granted. I had to represent my community well and all those people who would loved to have been on the road, whether advocating for others or just to see the country they love. The opportunity was similar to how I felt about the glorious and free living we have in Canada. Yes, we need to recognize that we have it good living in Canada, but we also need to be responsible and help maintain and extend that goodness.

Our time in the prairies built momentum for us heading into the last month of the run; however, there were still many tests and responsibilities ahead. We still wanted to reach our goals and tell thousands of people about Amy's story. We still had to climb the Rockies in order to dip our feet into the Pacific, and we wanted to raise as much money as we could for World Vision's Canadian partners. But the momentum we gained from the prairies made me believe more than ever in the mission of the run. I was leaving my doubts and my persistent ego behind. It was as if the jet stream had reversed its course and the wind was now at my back.

CHAPTER NINE: Here or There

IT WAS A BRUTAL HEAT WAVE. THE AIR WAS dry, and the ground was like dust. Clouds were barely forming. There had been no rain in months. Water supplies were in jeopardy of being lost for good. People were being forced to move from their homes and towns. The drought was the worst of its kind in decades. Animals were dying, millions of people were suffering and the young and the old were being threatened. This historical drought was in the Horn of Africa.

The drought affected the countries of Somalia, Eritrea, Djibouti, Kenya and Ethiopia. It began in June of 2011, and by August, it was a crisis requiring international emergency aid. World Vision Canada followed the lead of World Vision International and put all their fundraising efforts to the Horn of Africa from mid-August to mid-September. Unfortunately, it meant the cause of the One Nation Run was shelved for a month.

We understood why World Vision Canada made the decision. People's livestock and lives were in danger. Many had already died. World Vision Canada was also being directed by their international organization to make their sole focus the Horn of Africa. Because the Canadian wing of the organization was in a developed country, head office believed a generous Canada could greatly impact the region in their desperation. Other international organizations were following suit. The cry of the Horn of Africa was being heard by the world, and organizations were responding with compassion and relief. No complaints came from our team.

Yet as we crossed over the Saskatchewan-Alberta border, there were many cries from the children of Canada that were not being heard. Earlier in the year, a major flood caused an evacuation from homes and communities in many towns in Central Manitoba. The nation was not well-informed about how these remote communities were impacted. While we were on the road, not only had they been evacuated from their homes, but they still could not return to them. They were living in hotels and overcrowded motels in Winnipeg.

No media outside of Manitoba picked up the story. There was no major emergency aid given to the communities. There was no long term place to solve the problem of these communities faced, communities like Little Saskatchewan.

Another ongoing situation in over a hundred of these remote communities was the lack of clean water. CBC did a story on the problem while we were in Northern Ontario. The story seemed to go unnoticed by the Canadian public and was eventually overshadowed by the focus on the drought in the Horn of Africa.

The need for clean drinking water was just one of dozens of serious issues that needed immediate attention in these communities. Others included lack of access to education, unemployment, domestic violence, teen pregnancy, teen suicide and teen homicides. Children were sick, having babies and killing each other. This was happening in Canada – and it had been happening for the last two generations. The cries of these communities were not being heard, or at least few of them were responded to. Our team wrestled with the juxtaposition during the first week of September in Alberta. How could we as a country have a government, dozens of NGOs, church associations, school groups and other organizations be so focused on the Horn of Africa and not Central Manitoba? Why there and not here, too?

On August 31, our team arrived in Edmonton. Early that morning, before the day's relay, we dropped Marc off at the airport so that he could return to his family and his job. After the relay that day, we went to a barbeque in a park in the city, which was hosted by a group of high school students and their families. The team were to be the guests of honour. The students heard about our run in the spring through a World Vision Canada regional representative named Autumn, whom Zaya and I had met earlier that year.

Autumn had asked the group of a dozen students what project they would like to rally around for the remainder of 2011 and they picked our run. The students said they wanted to support our team because, "The stories of Canadian children who are really suffering are hidden. We do not want their story to be a secret anymore, and we want them to have the services and opportunities we have."

I was happy to call these students partners in our mission. What was unique about them was that the majority of them were either immigrants or second generation born Canadians. They knew the struggles of children and families in other countries. It could have been easy to pour money back to where their bloodlines originated, but they did not. It mattered to them that Canadian children were not left behind.

In the world of charity there is always a debate of "Here or There?" In the final month of our run, we were feeling the tensions of the debate, but as a team, we never believed that the focus should be about where to give, but rather on giving equally to the places of greatest need.

One piece of good news we received when we were in the Edmonton area was that we had reached one of our goals. We received a report from Genevieve from World Vision Canada that indicated we had reached over 100,000 Canadians with our message – mostly through media. The way Genevieve described our awareness success was, "If you guys were a YouTube video you would have had over 8 million views by now." Genevieve estimated that we had reached over 300,000 Canadians through our media interviews alone. It was an achievement we were proud of, especially since we had reached it four weeks before Vancouver. It certainly was confirmation for us that we had partnered with the right organization and confirmed our message was resonating with Canadians. But the numbers and goal reaching did not satisfy my soul.

While I ran through Alberta, there were quiet moments as I ran beside farm fields and towards the Rockies. I could not help but think about where Amy was and how she was doing. I thought about the children I met in Central Manitoba.

I knew I was in the right place, but my mind kept returning to the "Here or there?" debate. Would it not be more important to be with the children I knew? Would I not have a bigger impact if I focused my efforts on one community?

I thought about the questions that friends and strangers asked: *Couldn't you raise just as much money if you worked and gave all your money to the cause? How will your run benefit Amy? Do the kids you are running for even think your run is helpful? Why not pressure the government or partner with corporations?*

They were all good questions, some of which I asked myself. I weighed up the pros and cons but more than anything, I thought about Canadian children living in poverty. Thinking about where the children were and what their lives were like had me asking "Here or There?" I wanted to be with them, to help them, share their pain and also their joy. I wanted to understand more about the children and help them to paint a different picture for the future. In some respects, the questions I was asking were futile; I was in Alberta, and the road stretched out before me.

* * *

In Edmonton, our team dynamics changed dramatically. It was September, and we were on the eve of Labour Day weekend. My teammate Brittany needed to return to university. It was hard to say goodbye. She would meet us in Vancouver for the end of our run, but her absence for the next twenty running days would be difficult.

Brittany was not just the administrator on our team, she was a close friend. We had gone through the good, the bad and the ugly together. She was family.

We tried to be relaxed and practical about the change. However, for four months, we had shared almost every waking moment with Brittany. By the end of our four months together, I viewed her as my sister.

But Brittany needed to finish her degree in Early Childhood Education. Her studies would allow her to continue the type of work we were advocating for in Canada. Her experiences on the road solidified how meaningful her education was and how much her education could better the lives of Canadian families, especially the ones we were running for.

In the weeks following Brittany's departure, we were in constant communication through texts, Facebook messages and phone calls.

Brittany missed the camaraderie, the strong sense of purpose and daily goals. I also think she wanted to be on the road because she was falling more in love with her country. Most young adults want to take trips to California and Europe during the summer or after graduation; however, Brittany knew the trip would have a more important legacy for her as a citizen.

The morning after she left, Zaya and I woke up at 9:30 a.m., two hours late. The two of us debated whether Brittany should be "here or there." We had managed to stay up with our host later than usual and in doing so were too tired to hear the alarm. When we told Brittany about our lack of discipline without her, she scolded us like a mother – much deserved. Half joking, she asked us whether or not she should hop on a plane. To make up for our tardiness, we decided to do something that the run had yet to do: a "Trifecta."

In Edmonton, a good friend from Toronto joined the team. Her name was Heather, and she had been living in Edmonton for the last few years. When she heard about our run, she wanted to help. Heather was training for a marathon and decided she would use a long training run to help our cause. On August 31, Heather ran ten kilometres in our relay, then 30 kilometres on September 1.

Heather's 30-kilometre distance got us thinking. Instead of Zaya running 25 kilometres and me running two fifteen-kilometre runs, we decided to do 30-kilometre straight runs for the One Nation Run's first "Trifecta." Although my distance did not change, the fact that I was on the road for 30 kilometres in a row changed my mentality, making me more focused on the "here and now."

During the run, I pushed my pace a little faster than normal. It meant I had to think through my timing and my stride more. However, I also focused on who I was with and where I was more than usual. I thanked God for the position I was in, the places I ran through, the people who ran with me and those who supported us on the way. On the road, it was so easy to think about other people, the children who inspired us, my loved ones and those who we would speak to. On a run you could lose yourself and clear your mind of anxiety, this mentality was not always neces-sary, but a day after losing Brittany to school, missing Catherine and thinking about families who were suffering in the Horn of Africa and Central Manitoba, I needed to think more about "here" than "there."

We started the Trifecta at noon, and by sunset, Zaya had com-pleted his 30 kilometres. It was an amazing day of running. We danced to celebrate, and blared *John Legend and the Roots* from the SUV speakers. We then satisfied our hunger by eating out at another Indian restaurant. And then irony appeared in the form of a divine appointment.

Saturday, September 3 marked the first full day of the Labour Day weekend. Summer dreams were now coming to an end. The school break was on its last legs, and the return to the classroom was imminent. Zaya and I returned to the discipline of our run and shook off the cobwebs from a deep sleep, waking up at 6:45 a.m. to complete a combined 55-kilometre run. Before we exited the door of our hosts in Red Deer, I did a radio interview with a reporter from Calgary. In Calgary we would meet up with two friends, Will and Jeremy, who would be part of the team, Will for four and Jermey for two weeks respectively. But until then, Zaya and I would be the only members of the team.

In Red Deer, we would get some help running, as three children were set to run five kilometres. Zaya had finished his 25 kilometres for the day at 10:30 that morning. He ended in the heart of Red Deer on Highway Two. When Zaya was finished, he took a few minutes to stretch, hydrate and cool down. As Zaya cooled down, the three children and their mother pulled into the parking lot. The children were full of excitement. They popped out of the family van in running gear and smiles, laughing and asking us questions about our cross-Canada journey. In each of the children's hands was a sandwich bag containing money. Each child handed me a bag, and I asked them how much cash was there and where it came from.

The youngest girl chimed in, "This week, we went door-to-door asking our neighbours for donations for your cause." Zaya and I were caught off guard.

Then the little boy said, "Yes, we wanted to help the kids in need that you are helping."

We looked at each other, shocked by the children's personal fundraising. I imagined how easy it would have been for them to raise money, especially in their running gear and with their big smiles. I was not sure whether to cry or laugh. There was great irony in their action – two of the three children were adopted within the last year. Both adopted children were siblings from Ethiopia. My feelings of joy and the want to express them in tears or laughter must have been shared by God. I looked up into the sky and around me almost looking for a camera. Had God created a comedy with us in it? Had we just got "punked" by God?

For the last three weeks, World Vision Canada had been focusing all of their fundraising and relief work on the Horn of Africa, and now Zaya and I stood in the presence of two children from the Horn of Africa who had raised over 50 dollars with their Canadian-born sister for the neediest kids in Canada.

"Here or there" had just become "here meets there and there meets here." And maybe that was the point. Globalization had been making the world smaller by the decade in the last century, and now these two children just brought globalization right to our feet in a powerful yet ironic way.

No longer was charity about where someone lived. When someone's life begins to matter to you, you help them with whatever you have, regardless of where they are from. There were priorities that we believed as Canadians we needed to focus on, but in that moment with three children ready to run five kilometres as part of the One Nation Run, what mattered was that they had generous hearts and each one of them was willing to live out the good that was within them.

I watched the three of them run freely and happily. They ran together with a Canadian flag symbolizing their belief in the place they called home. At each water break, they buzzed with excitement to finish the five kilometres. I was speechless as I watched them, hoping that one day they could meet their peers who they would reach with their fundraising. It was one of the most memorable days of the run and one that still leaves me speechless. It was a beautiful story that could happen only in a few countries.

CHAPTER TEN: The Beginning in the End

THE SIGN READ, "THE MOST BEAUTIFUL Place on Earth", as we crossed into the province. With glacier rivers, massive mountain ranges and some of the largest trees in country, we were expecting British Columbia (BC) to live up to its sign; although as four Ontarians who grew up in the Toronto area, we had to laugh at BC's humility as our province is often labelled the most conceited. BC was the last province, the final frontier of the run, and I was glad to be in it.

As we entered BC, there was as much anticipation of the last province as there was the first. We had been on the road for over four months. We wanted to see the Pacific Ocean, we wanted to see another wonderful Canadian mega city and we wanted to run with young people on the seaboard of Vancouver. Yet I was missing Catherine. It had been over a month since I had seen her and because of the time difference we had not had a quality phone call in weeks. She would meet me in Vancouver in less than three weeks. There were many days that she was the biggest motivator to get me through the Rockies.

The Rocky Mountains were intimidating – a fence of spikes planted in our way. I thought they would be our biggest test. That was until we got some very interesting news from our hosts in Calgary: Calgary is 1,048 metres above sea level and Vancouver is approximately 100 metres above sea level. There is a 900-metre elevation difference between the two cities, which meant that even though we would have the three longest climbs of our trip through the Rockies that we would also have more declines than inclines. We certainly would still meet challenges, but we no longer had to think our times in the Rockies would be the most difficult – or all uphill – until Vancouver. In fact, the first two days after exiting Calgary we ran on either flat or downhill roads, which in some respects was more taxing on our joints on the steep slopes. There was another element of intimidation in BC: wildlife.

In Newfoundland we were warned by tourists and locals alike that there was great danger in driving at night. There are thousands of moose on the island and hundreds of near fatal or fatal accidents that happen annually. We were quite cautious when we drove the roads of "The Rock". In BC wildlife was a cause for concern because we were running mostly in mountain ranges and river valleys – two prime locations for bears and cougars, even in the day time. People told us not to worry, but instead, to be smart. For city boys, we were a little tense on solo runs. On the second day in BC as we ran through the skiing town of Golden, our fears took a definite shape.

The van was less than a kilometre ahead of me and before I arrived at the first water break on a clear-sky day, Will informed me that a cougar had just ducked into some brush a few metres from the road. He did not think there was a need to sound the alarm, but wanted me to be prepared nevertheless. I, however, was less than comfortable going toe to toe with a 90-pound predator and requested that the team travel behind me for the remainder of my run. At the second water break the team let me know that they saw two wolves on the edge of the forest, about 200 metres from where I was running. I was less frightened by the wolves in the daylight, but was happy to know that they had gone into the forest. I was not interested in any running competition. As the day progressed none of the other guys saw any wildlife. However, my heart rate was still quicker than normal when I began my afternoon run. After my first five kilometres I saw a mama bear and her cub crossing the road, probably returning to the forest after getting a drink from the Kicking Horse River. *I would have been less scared on a Kicking Horse*, I thought to myself. I immediately stopped and waited for the One Nation Run vehicle to get ahead of me. After the day in Golden the team and I never saw any dangerous wildlife close to the road, but it wasn't until we reached Kamloops the following week that I became less anxious to run in the mountains.

* * *

The great hospitality of ours hosts was continuous from Wanda's house in St. John's, NL to Calgary at the Fitch family residence. Our hosts in BC gave the same gracious attention to our team too. Was it a legendary as Newfoundland? You'll have to travel the country and be the judge of that. For us it was still worth writing home about. In Abbotsford a family we had never met let us stay in their home for five days while they were on vacation. Another family near Surrey reconfigured their main floor to accommodate our team. Other families saved up money to serve their best meal that month to us. The care we received left us in awe. But probably the most impressive response to Canadian hospitality that we heard was when we were near Revelstoke, BC, a small town in the middle of the mountains.

I was driving back to our accommodation when I saw a young man in his twenties hitchhiking. Usually on the road, I was unable to assist hitchhikers with no space in the vehicle, however, on this occasion, I pulled alongside him with an empty front seat. At the same time, another vehicle pulled up behind me. The hitchhiker said he was both hungry and wanting to go into town. Without hesitation I gave him some sandwiches left over from the run that day, while the woman from the car behind me, offered to take the man into town. The young man, who was a newly graduated university student from New Zealand said, "I love Canada. Everyone I meet is so kind. I feel like I am home away from home."

Through the interior towns of Revelstoke, Salmon Arm, Kamloops and Kelowna, we continued to tell the story of Canada's resilient yet neediest children. In BC I felt more confident when speaking to the media. When the One Nation Run began I had some national statistics, and the stories of the five remote villages in Central Manitoba to stoke the country to act, but when I reached the west coast I now had the country to speak about. When I spoke about Canadian child poverty I did so with some authority on the topic. I was able to give references to specific places that had been greatly affected and the reasons why. I also had countless conversations with people who were working on the front lines of poverty reduction in Canada; their own stories and experiences gave me answers I needed when peppered with hard questions. I also spoke with greater conviction and more belief that the work of ending child poverty in Canada had to be done, but more so, could be done. We had more faith and trust in Canada than ever before. My faith was not blinded by the beauty of the nation's natural resources. My trust was not derived from the gift of the adventure of a lifetime received by many generous Canadians, including my close friends with me on the road. No, my faith was in the leaders of the next generation, and my trust was in the foundation of compassion and justice that was established by past generations of Canadians.

On the second day in Kamloops I ended my running in the morning. World Vision had scheduled me to speak with five classes and a handful of university students over Skype. They were middle school and high school classes from Ottawa, Oakville, Winnipeg, Vancouver and Halifax. The university students were all from BC. The students listened to me for fifteen minutes as I spoke about how the trip was birthed and what the trip had been like, and then asked some general and specific questions about the adventure and mission of the One Nation Run. One university student then asked me two questions, passionately: "How can we put pressure on the government to change the future for those families living below the poverty line? What would you say is the number one issue facing families living in poverty?"

I wanted to ensure that all the questions asked by the students were given the respect that they deserved. This young lady's questions were important and I answered as best as I could. "As important as the government is, we need not place blame or pressure on it to be the primary group or institution that will provide the answers and solutions for child poverty in our country. Where we need to look first and foremost is in the mirror at ourselves, then with our families and neighbourhoods. When we look within, we will make the necessary changes within ourselves to find out who are in need closest to us and how we can help. I believe the government will follow its people.

"On the second question my answer would be affordable housing and if there is one area we could influence the government it would be on this very issue. Without a safe and affordable home to live in, families will not be able to make it financially and the stresses of finances will weaken the family unit where kids need nurturing the most. This issue affects Amy and other children living in isolated places the most as building and supply costs are highest there." My answers did not come from a trunk of responses that I randomly picked out of a pile, they came from the predominant feelings and research of experts in the field that I met from coast to coast. I was happy to share what I did and I was also proud of the university student for asking the questions and being engaged with the issues. When the energy and action of a country's youth are focused on the needs of the powerless, the country will move forward into prosperity.

The Okanongan Valley and Thompson County are considered to be the most unique and scenic areas in Canada. When we entered from the northeast corner and crossed the Shuswap River, we were amazed at its vegetation, as it boasted cacti, cherry trees and vineyards. The arid climate made sections of the area one of Canada's few deserts, adding another unique patch to Canada's quilt-like landscape. The dry conditions were easier on all of us as we ran. Most days were in the twenties and sunny, making it difficult for me to want to leave. The major urban centre in the Okanogan Valley was Kelowna, touted by locals as the most beautiful city in the country.

In Kelowna we would meet up with our friend Bethany Zeitner, who we met during our time in Antigonish, Nova Scotia. Bethany's family was hosting us while we spent three nights there. In Kelowna, Jeremy's time with us came to an end. He gave us consistency and an even-keeled manner, which earned him the nickname *Rock Steady*. Jeremy's departure left Will, Zaya and I to run the leg between Kelowna and Abbotsford. It was amazing to think that during the first week of the run we needed seven people to finish the 70-kilometre relay and during the final week we only needed three.

After some calculations at the Zeitner's home in Kelowna, I discovered the run was 160 kilometres ahead of schedule. Each day through the Rockies I had planned that the relay would travel 60 kilometres, thinking that the Rockies would push our limits. However, Zaya and my legs were strong enough to continue our 55 kilometre distance in BC. There was an emphatic "mm hmm" echoing from Ray Zahab. On top of that Will's enthusiasm pushed him from ten to fifteen kilometres during his second week with us. What this meant was that we needed to stay an extra night in Kelowna to avoid paying for another hotel room. As we found in so many hosts before them, the Zeitner's kindness accommodated us for a fourth night.

On September 22 we arrived in Hope, British Columbia – a small town at the foothills of the mountains. It is the gateway to the Lower Mainland of BC, and marked our last day of climbing or descending mountains. We truly were at the final stretch, only a day from the Great Vancouver area.

As beautiful as the mountains were and as iron like as our quads had become, I was ready for flat runs in the Lower Mainland. We had challenging runs in the Rockies of BC, two in particular. The first, near Revelstoke, was a steep ten-kilometre climb that led to Roger's Pass. That day Zaya and I ran together, against a steep incline and the perils of traffic. In the mountains there are no safe roads to run on, so our run up the mountain was on the shoulder of a major highway. The run up to Roger's Pass also went through short tunnels. We ran in the dark, up a steep mountain while cars were descending at a hundred plus kilometres per hour, and little over two metres away from us. It was a little unnerving.

On another run, just west of Kelowna, we ascended up a set of mountains for 26 kilometres straight. Will's fifteen kilometres that day were entirely uphill. We were not going to miss the mountains, but we sure did respect them.

* * *

Running through the lush, lower mainland reminded me of Nova Scotia, and being so close to the end reminded me about the beginning. When the three of us arrived in Abbotsford after a metric run, 100 kilometres, something Will wanted to do as he wanted to one up the Trifecta we had completed with Heather, we found ourselves significantly ahead of schedule. From where we were in Abbotsford to the Pacific Ocean was now only 80 kilometres. We took the next couple days to rest and celebrate. It was amazing to have two close friends with me, Will, who had known me since I was nine and Zaya, who I met in my late twenties and who shared a vision for Canada. In the coming days Catherine, Sim, Brittany and my parents would arrive in Vancouver for the final day of the One Nation Run, as well as other friends from back home. Flying across the country was a powerful sign of support.

The final day was Thursday, September 29. In many ways the last day was like the first in St. John's. There was no media coverage, a few local supporters and no hype. It felt like a running day with friends, only this was historic for us. We could not have asked for a nicer day. Unlike the fog of St. John's, the skies in Vancouver were clear and the sun warmly kissed our faces. Sim and Will began the day's relay running ten kilometres each. Then my friend Lisl who would host our team dinners while we were in Vancouver, ran seven kilometres with Catherine. Brittany and George, a friend from Toronto, ran with the two ladies for the last two and half kilometres.

Appropriately the last 30 kilometres were run by me and Zaya. Surprisingly Zaya did not want to savour the final run. Instead he pushed the pace. Zaya hit his running peak in Vancouver and used the final run as a tune up for the Toronto Waterfront Marathon that we and six other One Nation Run runners had signed up for as a victory lap. Because that is what you do when you are distance runners. I, on the other hand, had peaked somewhere in the prairies. I felt like Zaya's senior that last day in Vancouver with tired legs from downhill runs in the Rockies. As we flashed through neighbourhoods and market places from Burnaby to Kitsilano, the memories of the trip flashed through my mind. The land, the skies, the water, the homes, the food and the people all went through my mind like I was looking through a kaleidoscope. During our run that day I did not think about what we did or did not do or what we needed or wanted to do, I simply kept by Zaya's side and enjoyed the run. A kilometre from the end, Brittany joined us and we lightly jogged along Marine Drive as it curled around the west end of the University of British Columbia. Waiting at the end were the team of runners, my parents and my dad's cousin and his wife who lived in Vancouver. It was quiet, peaceful and it was a family moment. We hugged and congratulated each other.

The end of that day felt similar to the end of a lot of days of the One Nation Run. I was hungry, sweaty, in a great mood and with friends that were like family. We walked down a long set of stairs to Rec Beach, and dove into the water to cool off. While diving into the ocean that day I had officially travelled from Atlantic to Pacific, in total 126 running days from Signal Hill to Rec Beach. I stood up from the ocean and looked around, panning the view of the inlet. In the distance were mountains and the ocean stretching out over the horizon. As I looked in all directions to see the beauty and contemplate the moment, I recalled the last time I did the same thing; it was in Central Manitoba at a very rural intersection. The land was as level at a professional soccer field and snow covered. I stood there marvelling at the beauty and solace of the moment. It was my third trip to Central Manitoba and I needed that time to imagine something more for the children whose stories broke my heart. Now in Vancouver, having carried their stories across the country, I needed to pause again, this time with more confidence and more strength in what the future could be for Amy and her peers.

The next two days were spent eating and sleeping. I think it was possible our calorie deficiency was cancelled after the feasts we enjoyed at Lisl's house. We ate and laughed and shared stories from the run. At times, the conversation was serious and heart felt as we explained why we ran to Lisl's roommates and talked about children we met who inspired us. On the Saturday morning we got up early and arrived beside Vancouver's Science Centre for the One Nation Run celebration run event. The run was six kilometres and the route travelled the sea wall pathway ending in the famous Stanley Park. It was an odd experience for the team as there were microphones, One Nation Run posters and 30 or so other runners. The day had a similar feeling to that of our day in Montreal, but stark in contract to runs through the much of Canada where nature was our audience and companions. It was a lovely event put on by the Vancouver World Vision office. As was our team's custom we circled around with all present at the starting line and prayed thanking the Creator for life, breath, health and the opportunity to run freely. Joining us on the phone was a good friend of mine named Jobin Sam. Jobin and I had a few chats over the five-month journey. While I was on the road in Canada, Jobin was in Calcutta, India, teaching poor and blind children music and English. His partnership in advocating for and serving children living in poverty was life giving. It was incredible that I could celebrate that moment with him and we all could pray for him and the children he was with.

A horn sounded the run to begin and the thirty of us runners jogged along the sea wall trail. The light pace allowed Zaya and I to talk about our journey but also learn about the people we did not know who were running beside us. Beside me were three members of a local organization called Inner Hope. They were partners with World Vision Canada and were one of the benefactors of the One Nation Run fundraising. Two of the Inner Hope members, Jordan and Frankie, were young men who were participants of Inner Hope Ministries mentoring program. Jordan and Frankie were also aboriginal youth. As the four of us ran and shared stories I could not help but think about Amy and the dozens of other children I knew in Central Manitoba. When I met Amy she was six years old. Jordan was seventeen and Frankie was sixteen. Jordan and Frankie had both come from broken homes and difficult communities. Their parents struggled with addictions and their peers did not care much for education. Both young men carried with them a lot of anger and resentment when they first arrived at Inner Hope. Within a year they had both found success at school and forgiveness for their families and communities. What Inner Hope was providing for Jordan and Frankie was stability, support and a recovery of their imagination so they could dream about their future.

In many respects, Jordan and Frankie were the true realization of my dreams for the run and my dreams for Amy. The run was never about a journey I could experience or a bonding time that we could have. My dream was to tell Amy's story and see her life – and the lives of many others – matter to Canada as a whole. My dream was to see Amy healthy and attain a high school diploma before she would be pregnant. My dream for her was that she could dream about what she wanted her life to be and how she could help others in her community and province. To hear Jordan and Frankie speak elicited many emotions in me, but most importantly, it gave me a picture I could hold onto and share with Canadians. This picture mended the torn picture I had of Canada when I left Little Saskatchewan after my first visit.

CHAPTER ELEVEN:
The Power of Two

I AM ALWAYS INTERESTED IN HOW TWO people meet. From married couples, to acquaintances to good friends, I love to hear the stories and how their paths crossed. The closer the relationship, the more likely there is a twist in the story. Good relationships are precious, forged out of time and trust. The bond between two close friends is attractive to those who witness it and for me personally something I want to learn more about.

On the road, our team often asked our hosts how they met. We heard stories of married couples meeting for the first time and not liking each other, and stories of friends being thrown into times of stress. We were curious to know how their lives began together and what kept their relationship strong.

The run was now over. We had run in nine provinces for 126 days, while travelling 8680 kilometres. 330 people had participated in the relays of the One Nation Run, 119 households hosted our team and we were fed countless meals. We were interviewed on television 18 times, on radio 36 and 44 newspapers printed stories about the One Nation Run. And yet in Calgary, a seven-year-old girl only saw the importance of one thing.

"How did you two meet?"

Three days after the run officially concluded at Stanley Park, Zaya and I were in Calgary to give a presentation. I anxiously tapped on the steering wheel as we sat in rush hour traffic – nervous to be on time. We arrived at the school ten minutes early, like members of a boy band, wearing our matching Mondetta jackets. At the office, we were greeted by the physical education teacher who had invited us to the school.

"I am delighted you two guys could make it this morning. You have probably had a hectic schedule over the last week. How do you feel?

"We have a bit of a surprise for you that I am really excited about. You will not be speaking to a couple of older classes today. You will actually be speaking to all the classes from grade three to grade eight. Thanks again for coming."

When the teacher finished we looked at each other with a smirk on our face and the words, "expect the unexpected" echoing in our minds.

The students gathered in the gymnasium as the morning announcements had concluded. I was bursting with energy. It was the first time that either of us had spoken to this many students in person, since the run had begun. There was anticipation about the teachers. They seemed to be ready to hear our speech, as if it tied into their curriculum. The students packed the gymnasium like sardines in a can – squirming restlessly the way children do. The room buzzed with the soft electricity of expectancy.

We shared our stories of being children in Canada – two contrasting threads, weaving through the presentation. I started and Zaya spoke second.

"I was born near Toronto in a very good home and I had anything I needed or ever wanted," I said.

"I came to Canada at the age of seven with my family. We began in Montreal and I remember having to go to churches for extra clothes and meals," said Zaya.

"When I sang 'O Canada' at school I was so proud to be Canadian and the words could not have been truer," I said.

"I could not understand why there was so much hype about ice hockey and the Montreal Canadians," said Zaya.

As we took turns speaking, the students' eyes followed us back and forth like devoted tennis spectators. We needed to share what it was like for us to live in Canada. We wanted the students to relate to us so they could find themselves in our story. Once they were in our story they began to understand why we felt the way we did when we travelled to Manitoba and met Amy.

"There are thousands of stories like Amy's. There are children in Canada – the eighth richest nation in the world according to the United Nations Development Programme – who do not have clean drinking water coming out their taps, children are weak because their parents can't afford good food and there are even kids your age who no longer have hopes and dreams because they think life will never get better for them."

There was silence. The students' faces painted with disbelief that we were describing children's lives in Canada.

"But there is hope and the hope is in you. You can bring hope by becoming aware of those going through difficult times in your school and neighbourhood. Zaya's life and mine changed when we met Amy and got to know her and, when we became friends with her, she began to matter to us. And because she mattered to us, when she had problems in life, it mattered to us. The same will be true for you when you meet those near to you. When you make friends with those around you who are suffering you will want to help them out and make life better for them."

When our presentation was over, the physical education teacher came to the front and thanked us. He asked the students if they had any questions. One by one they excitedly raised their hands. At the beginning of the session many of the questions were about the run. The kids wanted to know how far we each ran, who was faster between us, and what area of the country was the most tiring to run through. They were also curious to know what was most challenging about our travels. We both said that being in close quarters with each other for six months was the greatest test. There was laughter at our teasing remarks. A few children asked questions about poverty in Canada and where Amy was now. Finally, the teacher said there was time for one last question. A seven-year-old girl stood up confidently and asked innocently: "Where did you two meet?"

It did not seem like the most important question to us, at the time. We were more interested in persuading students to make a difference and act compassionately in practical ways, and were hoping the students would ask questions about how they could end child poverty in their community. But when a hush came over the crowd to hear our answer, and we saw a keen interest from all the students, we both realized the significance of her question.

Zaya and I had met in October of 2005 through a student from the first church I pastored at. Zaya had met him at a camp where Zaya was the guest speaker. Knowing Zaya was interested in politics, sports and hip hop and was passionate about his faith, my student thought that we would get along. He was right. When we met, Zaya came to a small Bible study that I was hosting. He quickly became part of the discussion. Afterward he introduced himself to me. It was late in the evening and I asked him how he was getting home. He told me he was taking the bus and I asked if he needed a ride. We talked all the way home about many topics, from basketball to a trip I was taking to Rwanda later that fall.

"Hey man, I would really like to hear about your trip to Rwanda when you get back because Rwanda neighbours Congo where my family and I are from. It would be interesting to hear your thoughts about your time in the region."

We met up after the trip and talked about the history of the Great Lakes Region of Africa, about the hospitality of the people and how my trip impacted my view of life in Toronto.

"Did you eat all the food that you were served?"

"Of course it was delicious."

"Wow man, I am impressed."

"Well I have travelled a lot in my life."

"Tell me about it?"

Our discussions were often long. We liked to talk, but there was always a lot on our mind. Zaya and I would often talk about the difficulties in the world and in our communities. We wanted to see generosity and justice enter into each person we knew and into our neighbourhoods. We also made sure we balanced our discussions with some light hearted stuff by watching or playing sports.

Like most friendships ours centred on our interests and passions. We talked about what mattered to us; we built trust with each other, and we had fun. There was nothing forced about it even though we were intentional in what we did and talked about. Being friends with each other made sense and came naturally.

However, the young lady asking the question had something else in mind when she asked it. Although young, she was insightful to see things we were not always aware of or at least did not make into a barrier between us. She saw that we were different and that our stories were different and she wondered how two guys of different races, cultures and economic backgrounds, could become such good friends so quickly.

In Marshall McLuhan's words: "The medium is the message. The form of information or truth that is revealed by someone holds more significance than in its content." To that young lady, we were the message, and what we said only mattered because it was part of who we were. When we were travelling across Canada asking children to be aware of those who are around them that are different and make friends with them, we thought the challenge was important. When we said to children, "Make friends with those who are going through difficult times so that their difficulties matter to you and you can be part of the solution or healing needed in their life," we thought the message was true and powerful for social change because of the content we presented. What we failed to realize was how important our stories were and how important our friendship was as we communicated our message. When kids saw us they listened to what we had to say, but the impact of our decision to be friends and run across Canada together was more powerful. In seeing us as friends they had a model to begin social change.

Zaya answered the girl's question, first with humour and then with heart. He talked about us arguing about when and how we met. (The story I wrote in this book is not the story he would tell you. For that story you will just have to meet Zaya for yourself.) He then said I was crazy, but that I was crazy about being compassionate. He talked about us finding a brother in each other despite our differences.

Later that day when we were driving from Calgary to Regina, there were many moments of silence or just listening to music. We looked at the unique topography of the prairies and endless acres of farmland, and we thought about our runs through Saskatchewan and the relief we had of not having to run into the 60-kilometre wind gusts. We remembered how long we had journeyed together over the last six months, and, the last six years. And we marvelled at the insight of that girl. In many ways she had left us speechless, a difficult task to say the least. The One Nation Run was birthed after meeting a little girl. Now it had been summed up through the observation of another.

When we woke up the next day in Regina, we went for a fifteen-kilometre run. It was like a cool down from those in the previous week. But like so many others, it was as much for our minds as it was for our bodies. As we ran we laughed about me locking the keys in the car the evening before and some of the other misadventures we had had over the course of last six months. I thought back to the moments we had shared – just the two of us. They were moments that prepared us for interviews, calmed us down from hectic days and gave us clarity of what we were doing and why we were doing it.

It would be a difficult transition to be in one place for more than a week. We were now so used to being nomadic that being settled in one location would be unsettling. When someone has been on a treadmill for an hour and then gets off it is difficult to stand on solid ground. There is a feeling that you are still in motion and a feeling you should still be moving. Yet the closer we got to Southern Ontario, the more I knew what would be the hardest aspect of transition from life on the road. It was something Brittany and many others had felt who travelled with us for more than a couple days. The most difficult part of life back home was going to be living without each other.

When you begin a friendship with someone, you find you have things in common and trust is established. The longer you spend being friends, the more moments you share, the more trust you build, the stronger that friendship becomes. Your friend's life becomes part of yours and they matter more to you day by day. Before Zaya and I started the One Nation Run, we were close friends and saw each other like brothers. Life on the road was not always easy; there were times we annoyed each other and needed a few kilometres to run off a disagreement. But for the most part, the other guy was the most important person we had for six months. If there was disharmony between us, or either of us struggled for any reason, we felt it even more. Our friendship meant that if there was something worth celebrating in that person's life we could celebrate with them fully. Their joy was our joy. Their pain was our pain.

That is why we challenged people to become friends with those different than themselves and urged people to become friends with those who were going through hard times in life. We wanted their ups and downs to matter to each other. When people matter to you, you respond to them quickly and in the way they need you most. Problems still exist, but they are easier to deal with because you are facing them together.

Without question, our challenge was idealistic. It carried an unrealistic altruism with it. We were asking people to stretch out and become friends with people that were different from them, and where there are differences there are often barriers. Maybe that is why we challenged and encouraged children first and foremost. Their imaginations can often carry this same unrealistic altruism. A child's imagination can take hold of realities that seem impossible. It was a teenager that had the imagination to believe Zaya and I would become good friends. It was children that pushed Zaya and I to dream bigger for our country. It was and will be children who will live out this dream daily. It will be children who will have the imagination to make Canada better even on its darkest days.

CHAPTER TWELVE: Where do we go from here?

WHEN I RETURNED TO SOUTHERN ONTARIO, friends and family members were glad to see me. I was touched by how many of them had followed the One Nation Run on line, supported us in prayer and shared with friends and co-workers the stories of those we were running for. When I returned, people had many questions they wanted to ask me, yet the most common question was: "Are you exhausted after all that running?"

I tried to be honest, but when I answered, most people were surprised, confused or perhaps even thought I was being arrogant. My honest response was: "The easy part was the running. The hard part really begins now."

I love to run. I enjoy the sweating, the freedom, the challenge of inclines, the fresh air even when it is cold – cold weather for avid runners is like cold water for avid swimmers, once your in it for a few minutes its really no big deal –, the clarity it brings the mind, the time running alone or the friendship if I am running with someone else. In the last fourteen years that I have focused on running I have always enjoyed it. The same was true on the One Nation Run. I had nervous moments because of British Columbia's wildlife and the seclusion of Northern Ontario weighed on my city-boy mind at times, but for the gross majority of the 127 running days, I loved it. No matter how hot, how cold, how wet, how foreign the towns or how busy the streets, I loved running across Canada and usually was not any more tired after a run than someone finishing a gym class or a long leisurely bike ride. So when I answered people I can see why they were confused, surprised or thought I was being arrogant; however, I was being truthful.

The One Nation Run as a whole, however, was not just about running. It was a mission and a media stunt, a method in which the team and I could get people's attention to tell the story of Amy and others. Some people choose to protest for their cause, while others choose to jump into cold water, some bake and others tweet. I believed running across Canada would get people's attention the most. But now that the run was over and few people were going to pay much attention while I cooked, cleaned and went to work, would people or media outlets still care about the story I wanted to tell? If I decided to host an event or show up at someone's school to tell the story of the children and didn't tell people I ran across Canada, would anyone show up or anyone listen? I wanted to say yes. I wish I could say that that was the case, yet, the truth was that now that the run was over, I had to look in the mirror and ask myself the question: "Where do you go from here?"

The question was actually being asked on the road by certain reporters and families when we arrived in the prairies, "So Bryce, when the run is over what will you do?" We had asked each other that question, too. We knew there would be more after the run, but *what* and *where* and *how* were not questions that we had answers to. The run was never going to be the ending. Like Terry Fox and Rick Hansen with their runs, I never saw the One Nation Run as the end or believed the conclusion of it would solve the problem. And the One Nation Run certainly did not end child poverty.

When we got into a van heading to St. John's, we did so with a cause we believed in. Our message was primarily told on the roads we ran on and in the homes we ate and slept in. Our goal in getting into people's homes was to voice the stories of the most vulnerable children so that Canadians would be confronted with Canadian child poverty. We wanted people to think when they turned on their taps that in Canada there were those who did not have clean drinking water. We wanted them to open their fridge and know that there were kids in their country who did not have food in their fridges. We wanted our hosts to see that their needs were being met and to know that together we could meet every Canadian child's needs, starting with the one closest to them. We knew that not every family would know children living in poverty in their town or city, so we thought we would introduce their reality to our hosts. The challenge we gave to each family after we told the stories was: "You have now hosted us, strangers, in your home and you took care of us like family and made sure all our needs were met. Now we ask that you look for children and families on hard times in your town and invite them in and help meet their needs." We knew the message was idealistic, the message required people to change their lives. We knew it was not an easy message to live out, but we knew if it was put into practice then relationships would be the antidote to the disease of poverty.

The word compassion is made from two Latin words, cum and passus. The word cum in Latin means "with" and the word passus means "to suffer." Compassion literally means "to suffer with." In its literal meaning, compassion is challenging to live out. It demands a change in someone and an action toward someone else. When I grew up I thought being compassionate meant to be worried or concerned about another person or to have pity for someone. Compassion was a feeling I had, like when a neighbour's father died or school mate was bullied. But I believe that compassion's literal meaning is far more useful and necessary in life and in ending Canadian child poverty. The literal meaning was what I used when I asked myself or was asked the question:

"Where do you go from here?" I believe the answer to the question is to show compassion, meaning after the run I needed to continue to suffer with people – to make their pain my pain. The One Nation Run was a step of compassion. I suffered with the children of Canada by giving up the life I knew and running in solidarity with those in need and being a voice to the voiceless. Now I needed to take the next step. But what would that be? It felt like I had just returned from Central Manitoba after meeting Amy for the first time.

Since I was twenty years old I have had four role models of compassion. Three of them were Mother Teresa, Ghandi and Dr. Martin Luther King. What was amazing about all three was that they all shared a role model who also happens to be my greatest role model in being compassionate, Jesus. Jesus is the greatest person of compassion in my opinion, because of how far He went "to suffer with" those in need. In all of my role models of compassion there is a distinct change in their life when they decided to be compassionate in a mission. Ghandi moved back to India and lived a simple life like a fellow Indian peasant on top of confronting the empire that was oppressively ruling over his people. Mother Teresa gave up the opportunity to have a family of her own and moved to Calcutta, India, to make the children and families who were hurting most to be her family. Dr. King led the civil rights movement in the United States and travelled all over the country to motivate and inspire people, even facing physical and legal punishment. Jesus showed radical inclusion to all people, breaking social and religious barriers and for that he was punished and died a criminal's death. Yes, they saw people hurting and that caused their emotions to change, but compassion did not truly begin in them until they decided to act and change their lives in order "to suffer with" those who were hurting.

I realize as I write, that compassion seems to be extreme. My role models were some extremely brave people who are seen as some of the most benevolent beings in human history. But there are ways that they began being humane before their lives dramatically changed. Three simple acts of compassion is what I started with in 2008, when first meeting the children of Central Manitoba. They are the same three acts I would return to when I finished the run and the three acts I will challenge you with, too.

The first is act of compassion is to be generous. When people think of being generous they often think of giving money. There are other ways of being generous too. Basically generosity is giving anything you own or have to someone else and I think all forms of beneficence are important to remember; however, I do want us to think about giving money first. When I met the children of Central Manitoba I wanted to fix their problems and rescue them from their situation. It was not the best perspective to have, but that was my initial response. I understood that I did not live near them, but I knew I could help from a distance and so I gave a donation to Rick and Liz and their mission in helping the kids to be kids for a day. In giving money we must see how it is an act of compassion to experience its full weight. In giving money to someone or spending money to help meet the needs of someone, not only are you giving something but you are also limiting the amount of money you have and in turn, limiting how much you can possess. In a small way you are being compassionate, because you are choosing to experience a fraction of what someone else is suffering in. You are limiting your spending freedom. I think this is a good discipline for us to have in being charitable, especially in Canada where we often have more than we need. In giving or using our money for someone else, we restrain from buying the latest gadget or clothing item or anything else that is extra, above our needs. It means that we will choose not to keep up with all the trends and some peers, but it does mean someone else has a Christmas gift or can afford to go to the dentist or provide for countless number of needs.

The second act of compassion is listening to a person's story. In understanding poverty there is a dominant assumption that people make. They believe that those in poverty have made decisions to put themselves and their family in the position they are in. Three comments I want to make on that before we continue on the second step of compassion. First, it is never a child's fault that they are in poverty. It is frustrating when we see an adult put their child in a vulnerable position when we think it is avoidable, but to punish the child by focusing on what the parent has done is not protecting or helping the child. Second, we all make bad decisions throughout our lives, and a lot of times when we make a bad decision, there are people in our lives who help us out of the situation we have put ourselves in. In writing this book I made many mistakes and, if it was not for friends of mine, I would not have been able to finish and publish my story. Finally, sometimes bad things happen to good people. There are many families living one step away from the poverty line and if they lose their job, get sick or an accident occurs, they could easily fall into poverty from no fault of their own. Canadian children and families living in poverty are people first, not a statistic or the numbers they have in their bank account. By listening to their story you can find out how or why they are in the difficulties they are in and you can find out if they need help. More than anything else, in listening to their story without judgement you can help them restore their dignity. A relationship with someone who cares might be the greatest gift they can receive, as they no longer have to face poverty on their own.

The third act of compassion and the final one I will challenge you with is advocating. After you listen to a friend, child or family's story there is a next step. This next step is the most difficult, but it will become a lighter load as you practice the second step more. When you hear someone's story face to face you have begun a relationship with that person. In a relationship the person will begin to matter to you to a greater extent. Advocating is not easy, but when it is done for someone who matters to you, the desire to help is bigger than the discomfort or fear you may have. When you advocate for someone else you are choosing to stand with them in their struggle. In some cases, it will be defending them from mockery. In other cases it might be to walking to the office of a local leader, whether religious, political or civic, and asking them what they are doing to reduce child poverty and how you can help or it could simply be asking your parents if you could make a second lunch and bring it to your friend at school. With the story of the person you know in your heart you will no doubt have all the inspiration you will need to stand up and stand with them against their problems.

These three simple acts of compassion, giving money, listening and advocating are the building blocks of compassion. You will come back to these steps every time you are confronted with an injustice or struggle facing someone near to you. All my heroes of compassion returned to these steps over and over again even when they were leading local or national movements of justice and peace.

When the One Nation Run came to a conclusion, I first returned home to Mississauga to enjoy a Thanksgiving meal with my family. Catherine was there to meet me. The weekend was a celebration as we were all together. Later that weekend I moved back to Ottawa from the One Nation Run, yet I had three specific things to do. First, marry Catherine. Second, write a book about the One Nation Run and finally, return to the building blocks of compassion within my neighbourhood and city.

On November 26, 2011, behind the Supreme Court of Canada, I got down on one knee and proposed to Catherine. That night she said yes and on December 30, 2011, in front of 30 friends and family members, half dozen of whom viewed the wedding on Skype from Jamaica, Catherine and I became husband and wife. I could not have been happier. I now got to share my vision and dreams with my best friend and adventure with her in life.

When Catherine and I returned from our honeymoon in Prince Edward County, Ontario, I began writing this book, a challenge Zaya gave to me at the beginning of the run. I guess I figured saying yes to his challenge was the least I could do after he travelled across the country with me for six months. The book went through many drafts and revisions. It was a challenge I was nervous about and struggled through as I do not find that I am a gifted writer. I knew in writing the book it would, at the very least, be a gift to Zaya along with all those who journeyed with us on the road, whether for a kilometre or an entire province. We both hoped that the book would be able to get the story of the most vulnerable children into more Canadian homes.

The third task was the most difficult for a handful of reasons. How could I speak to students about being compassionate in their neighbourhoods if I did not do this as well? I remember being with a high school drama class in Orleans, Ontario, that was working on a humanitarian focused performance with World Vision called "The Other Side of the River". One of the students asked me bluntly in front of all his class mates during a Q and A session: "How are you going to reduce child poverty now?" It was a question that comes most often when children are being advocated for: "Sure you helped one kid or kids for one year, but don't you have a heart to continue to be compassionate for them?" I answered with sincerity and told the student that for now, I was writing a book and meeting my neighbours. The answer did not give the student the resolve he was looking for, but I was being honest, nevertheless.

I knew that my neighbourhood was where I had to start. It was not flashy or world changing, but it was where I needed to begin again in a new city and in a new neighbourhood. I began acting by simply keeping my ears and eyes open to find out who was hurting, stressed, lonely or going through transition.

In being compassionate there often exists a myth that one person gives and the person in need receives. This is simply not true. When a person reaches out to another they receive just as much if not more. Ask anyone who has been on a building project in a developing country or to a downtown soup kitchen, or ask any of my friends who visited Central Manitoba. The person of compassion receives humility, a lesson on what matters most and builds a relationship with someone different than themselves, which enriches their life. In the movie *The Blind Side*, Sandra Bullock's character Leanne Touhy, sums up the reciprocal nature of the relationship of compassion. The story of *The Blind Side* is about a wealthy family who takes in a teenage boy named Michael, who has recently become homeless. Leanne cares for Michael as best she can, treating him like her own son. The Touhy family then adopts Michael with his permission. During a conversation over lunch with a few friends at a private golf course, one of Leanne's friends says to Leanne: "What you are doing for this boy is changing his life." Leanne then quickly responds: "No, by taking care of Michael he is changing me."

If you have seen *The Blind Side* it is obvious that the Touhy family made a significant, positive impact on Michael's life. Michael was given a home, new clothes, and a driver's license, graduated high school, received a full football scholarship and had a stable family who he could love and that loved him unconditionally. But there were many ways Michael changed Leanne and the Touhy family in a positive way, too. The Touhys became more generous, less superficial, more grateful and became closer as a family. When we choose to make friends with children and families who are hurting or going through struggles, we then see how resilient they are, how happy they can be with very little, and how much they appreciate people's kindness. Those who are experiencing economic difficulties, understand the value of a dollar and the value of a person. So, if you are wealthy – or are at least wealthier than a child or family you are being compassionate toward – there is a powerful exchange that takes place between both parties. As Shane Claiborne writes in his book Irresistible Revolution': "I truly believe that when the poor meet the rich, riches will have no meaning. And when the rich meet the poor, we will see poverty come to an end."

Opening your life and home is testing, especially to neighbours you do not know well or complete strangers. It is something you have to live out with wisdom, along with love and courage. I know as you are compassionate you will positively impact the life of a child or family. I know you, too, will receive inspiration, renewed appreciation for life and will gain new friendships. But more will take place around you. The effects will spread to others. Your friends will be watching you and maybe at first they will think you are being foolish or going through a phase, but as you reach out, they too will be changed. And when the waves of compassion make contact to the hearts and minds of your peers, the sound of the national anthem will echo louder and louder in our country and you will begin to see how great the song of Canada really is: "Oh Canada" is best when its lyrics are experienced within Canada's borders.

When I think about the children I ran for, specifically Amy, I realize it is difficult to reach out to her as I live in Ottawa. I am not sure if I will ever meet her again. I know I could if I wanted to. I could ask Rick and Liz to join them for a week in the summer or be part of their now annual winter road trip. But whether that would be for her or for me, I don't know. From time to time I will ask Rick and Liz how Amy's community is and if they have seen her. I pray for her often. I know life is hard for her community and that the problems that she faces are not going to go away anytime soon, as the conditions she lives in are a result of over a hundred years of bad decisions and mistakes, of which none were her fault. I pray that she can break the cycle of poverty for herself and her children and I believe Rick and Liz are helping Amy and her community each day by doing what they are doing.

When I first reached out with Rick and Liz I had no idea it would impact me the way it did. I had no way of knowing how much Amy would change my life. I simply wanted to let her know that she was not alone in her struggle and that other Canadians cared. But that is the power of compassion, it ties people closer to one another and those who you are tied to matter more. I am not sure if Amy knows her story carries so much inspiration. Maybe one day I will meet her again and tell her how her story carried me across the country.

And now like the One Nation Run, my section of the run is over. It does not mean that I will stop running or being compassionate or an advocate for the most vulnerable where I am, but it does mean it is time for another runner to take the torch.

In writing this book I intended to write to a teenage audience because for one, I love teenagers, but I also love their keen interest in acting out what they believe. Maybe in writing for a teenage audience I wanted to speak to the teenager in all Canadians. Within us we all have a place in our beings that wants to act and no longer talk about or imagine something. So this is my formal invitation to you. It is your turn to act, to take the torch of compassion and advocacy and continue the work that so many Canadians have done before you.

When I speak to young Canadians about their involvement in ending child poverty in Canada I tell them three things: First, you are needed in this fight; second, you are gifted beyond belief for the fight and, finally, you are trusted to fight. These words are for you as well.

Initially when I began to advocate for Amy and her peers I had nothing more than who I was, the community I was in, and the job I held. But I realized that in me, my network and my position, I had all that I needed. The same is true for you. You have more than enough to begin running and doing the work of ending child poverty. And like me, as you run and strive to bring Canadian children what is rightfully theirs, a glorious and free life, you will find that you are not running alone and that you can reach the distant goals you have set out before you.

REFERENCES AND
FURTHER STUDY LIST

Bibliography (statistics and quotes cited from the following resources)

Assembly of First Nations, Technical Bulletin: Safe Drinking Water for First Nations Act – Bill S-8, November 2013

Claiborne, Shane, Irresistible Revolution, Zondervan, 2006

Gourevitch, Phillip, We Wish to Inform You That Tomorrow We Will Be Killed With Our Families: Stories From Rwanda, Macmillian, 1999

Hancock, John Lee, The Blind Side, Alcon Entertainment and Fortis Films, 2009

Legend, John and The Roots, Wake Up!: Wake Up Everybody, GOOD and Columbia, 2010

LL Cool J, Mama Said Knock You Out: Around the Way Girl, Def Jam Recordings, 1990

Mandela, Nelson, Make Poverty History Address, Trafalgar Square, London, England, 2005

McLuhan, Marshall, Understanding Media: The Extensions of Man, McGraw-Hill, 1964

Newfoundland Department of Environment and Conservation, www.env.gov.nl.ca, 2010-2013

Shad K, The Old Prince: Get Up, Black Box Recordings, 2007

Statistics Canada, www.statcan.gc.ca , 2010-2013

United Nations Development Programme, hdr.undp.org, 2010-2013

Wikipedia (for general information), www.wikipedia.org 2010-2013

World Vision Canadian Programs, Poverty at Your Doorstep, World Vision Canada, 2013

Further Study List (put together by Bryce Dymond and Zaya Kuyena)

Note: Those resources with a star beside them are for mature audiences. Those under 18 should dialogue with their parents/guardians prior to reading, viewing or listening.

Reading

*(The) Book of Negroes by Lawrence Hill, Canadian author

Chief: The fearless vision of Billy Diamond by Roy MacGregor, Billy Diamond was the Grand Chief of the Grand Council of the Crees from 1974 to 1984

Free The Children by Craig Kielburger, Craig is co-founder of Free the Children

Heart Matters by Adrienne Clarkson, Former Governor General of Canada

*(The) Oredna by Joseph Boyden, Professor of Creative Writing and Aboriginal History

(The) Power of Generosity by Dave Toycen, President and CEO of World Vision Canada

Seven Generations by D.A. Robertson and Scott B Henderson, a graphic novel series for younger readers

Shattered by Eric Walters, one of Canada's most popular youth and children's writers

Terry by Doug Coupland, a biography of Terry's Marathon of Hope

Viewing

*Cry Freedom, movie about South Africa's apartheid, starring Denzel Washington and Kevin Kline

Ghandi, biopic about the life of Mohandas Ghandi, starring Ben Kingsley

(The) Great Debaters, starring Denzel Washington

Hi-Ho Mishtahey, a documentary about Attawapiskat children longing for better education

Listening

Arcade Fire
A Tribe Called Red
Billy Talent
Ceremony
Couer de Pirate
Fiest
K'Naan
Sarah Harmer
Shad K